Arta
The Scre
Body

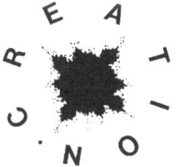

CREDITS

THE SCREAMING BODY

Stephen Barber

ISBN 1 84068 091 1
Copyright © Stephen Barber 1999
First published by Creation Books 1999, reprinted 2001
New edition published 2004
www.creationbooks.com

Cover design: The Tears Corporation
All illustrations by courtesy of the owners
Sorcellerie Et Cinéma and *La Révolte Du Boucher*
copyright © Editions Gallimard, Paris, 1978

Acknowledgements
For their help and generous encouragement, I want specially to thank Marianne
Alphant and Germain Viatte of the Centre Georges Pompidou and its National
Museum of Modern Art in Paris, and Antoine Coron of the
National Library of France.
For assistance of varying kinds, I also thank: in Paris, Philippe Sollers, Julia
Kristeva, Jacques Derrida, Pierre Guyotat, Albert Dichy, Alain Cuny, Claude
Autant-Lara, Henri Chopin, Clotilde Milliex, Chantal Thomas, Allen Weiss,
Clayton Eshleman; in Vienna, Hermann Nitsch, Ursula Krinzinger, Leo Navratil,
Johann Feilacher; in Tokyo, Eikoh Hosoe, Akiko Motofuji, Kazuo Ohno,
Kuniichi Uno, Min Tanaka, Tadashi Uchino; in Berlin, Peter Chevalier, Salomé;
in New York, David Frankel, Ingrid Sischy, Raphael Rubinstein, Patti Smith; in
London, Stephen Bann, Malcolm Bowie, Jeremy Reed, John Maybury, Jane Giles.
Much of this book is based on interviews over many years with the two people
most important to Artaud at the end of his life – Gaston Ferdière, who died in
December 1990, and Paule Thévenin, who died in September 1993.
Artaud loathed the first and loved the second.
All translations of Artaud's words in this book are my own.

CONTENTS

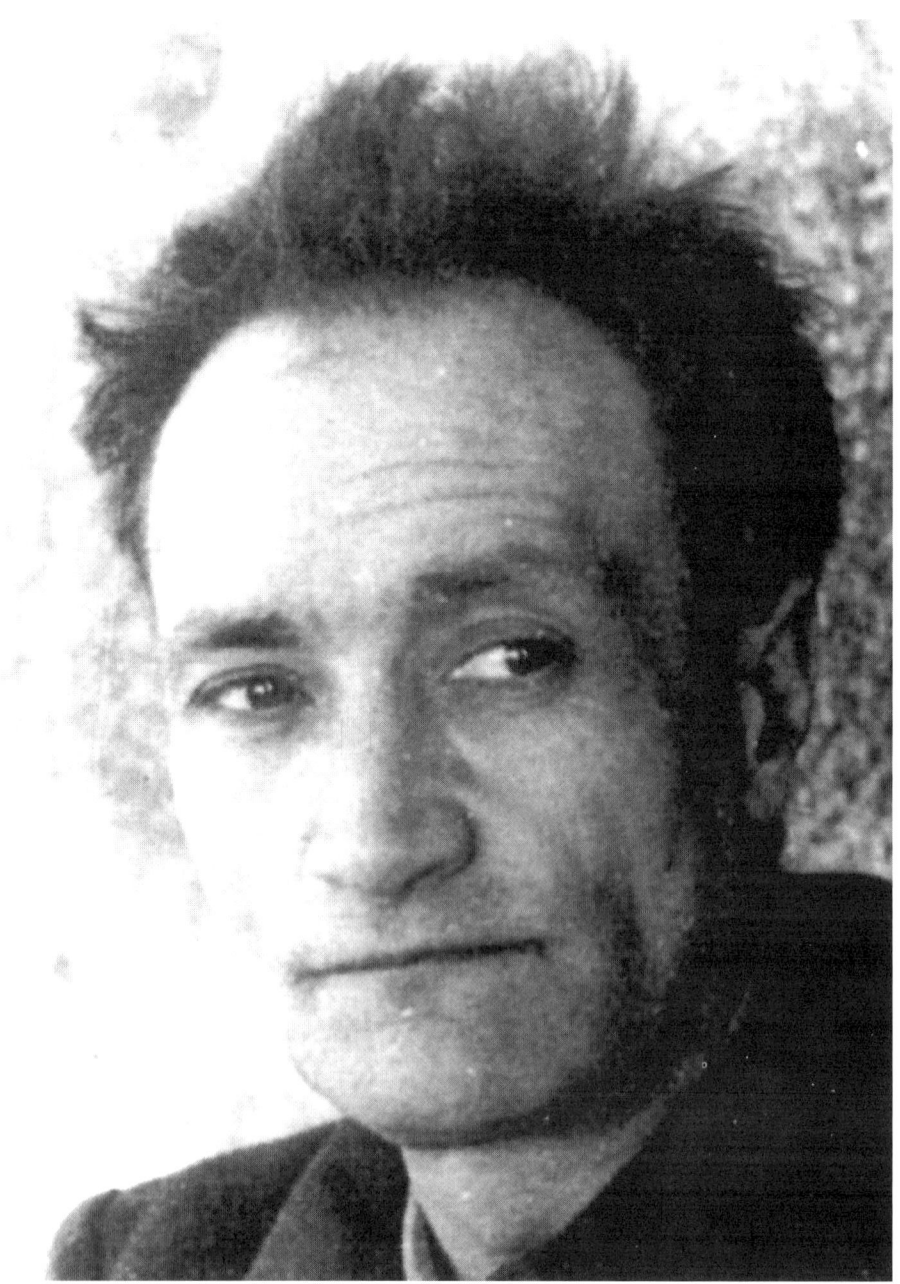

Antonin Artaud at Rodez asylum, 1946

Introduction

The impact of the work of Antonin Artaud in the fields of art, writing and performance has been colossal, expanding and multiplying its potential as time sifts through its repercussions and ricochets, and as previously unknown work has been made available. Artaud's acutely lucid investigations into the nature of language and representation, of society and madness, and of the human body and gesture, have all proved extraordinarily seminal, especially in French theoretical work from the mid-1960s to the present, in the writings of such figures as Jacques Derrida, Gilles Deleuze and Julia Kristeva.

In the 1960s, it was Artaud's theatrical work – the theory and imagery of the "Theatre of Cruelty" – which proved a huge source of world-wide inspiration for experiments in theatrical form and staging. But in more recent years, it has been Artaud's non-theatrical work which has provoked the most intense attention. Exhibitions of his drawings have been held in Paris, at the Centre Georges Pompidou, in 1987 and 1994; in Marseilles, at the Musée Cantini, in 1995; in New York, at the Museum of Modern Art, in 1996; and in Vienna, at the Museum Moderner Kunst, in 2002. Retrospectives of Artaud's work in cinema have been held in Paris, at the Centre Georges Pompidou, in 1987, and in London, at the National Film Theatre, in 1993. And Artaud's recorded work for radio – notably his incendiary final project of screams and protests, *To Have Done With The Judgement Of God*, which was completed only six weeks before his death and whose transmission was prohibited – has been issued in its entirety on compact disc in France, in 1995. All of these manifestations of Artaud's previously hidden or inaccessible work have accentuated the need constantly to re-assess and interrogate his language and images as new, intersecting constellations.

This book solely concerns Artaud's non-theatrical work. It explores his work in cinema in the 1920s and early 1930s and his attempts to find filmic forms for his theories of cinema, which directly prefigure his subsequent work in the areas of drawings and recordings. The book investigates the intricate trajectory of Artaud's drawings – from intentionally decimated magic "spells", to fragmented imageries of the human body executed in a lunatic asylum, and ultimately to facial portraits conceived as raw excavations of human identity. Finally, the book examines Artaud's recorded work of the end of his life as the most intensive realization of his plan to anatomize and recast the entire conception of the human body. This is one of the most astonishing, extreme and radical projects in the culture of the twentieth century. All of Artaud's visual work is multi-dimensional, both ferocious in its anti-social polemic and densely nuanced in its visual texture. Even Artaud's scream, as this book will show, is visual in intent: a visualization of the human body as Artaud projected it, in his uniquely ambitious and challenging final work.

One

Extremities of the Mind: Artaud's Film Projects 1924–35

Artaud devoted a great deal of his time to cinema projects in the years between 1924 and 1935, from the ages of twenty-eight to thirty-nine. He wrote fifteen film scenarios in all, and was the only one of the writers associated with the French Surrealist movement to produce a body of theoretical work about the potential of cinema. But despite his expansive engagement with cinema, it is the crucial area of his production which has remained most closed to investigation. To some extent, this is the result of the fragmentary and scattered nature of Artaud's theoretical writings on the cinema, and of the relentless calamities he faced in attempting to make films that could embody his revolutionary theories for cinema. One particular factor in this occlusion has been that Artaud is known as having written the scenario for one of the three great examples of Surrealist cinema, **The Seashell And The Clergyman** (the other two being Luis Buñuel's **Un Chien Andalou** and **L'Age d'Or**), but this is a film which has acquired an ambiguous and contradictory reputation. In contrast to Buñuel's two films, it is very rarely seen. The film baffled most viewers whenever it was screened in Britain and the United States, largely due to the intervention of a disruptive element of chance which would certainly have pleased the Surrealists, if not Artaud himself. When the reels of the film were first sent from France to the United States for distribution, they were re-assembled by error in completely the wrong order. The version of the film which resulted is the one which has been most prominently distributed in the United States and Britain from the late 1920s to the present. The incoherence of the work certainly contributed to the censorship initially imposed upon the film by the British Board of Film Censors, which used the justification: "The film is so cryptic as to be meaningless. If there is a meaning, it is doubtless objectionable."[1]

A further factor in the reputed distancing of **The Seashell And The Clergyman** from Artaud's own intentions lay in the dispute over the gap between text and image that flared up between Artaud and the film's director, Germaine Dulac. The film acquired the reputation in the late 1920s of having been steered away from its original conception by Dulac, to the detriment of the project. Artaud had originally intended to direct his scenario himself, but failed to find the funding to do so. As a result, he deposited the manuscript of the scenario, which he had written in April 1927, at an institute where film producers could look at scenarios with a view to acquiring the rights to film them. Dulac found the scenario there, and decided both to produce and direct the film herself. Dulac was already a legendary figure within experimental film circles – a prolific member of the group of French film-makers known as the Impressionists, which included Abel Gance, and the only female film-maker working in France at the time. Although Artaud had been expelled from the Surrealist movement by its leader André Breton in November of the previous year, his association with what remained at the time an extremely fashionable movement convinced Dulac of the objective challenge to be faced in attempting, for the first time, to make a "surrealist" film work.

When **The Seashell And The Clergyman** went into production in the summer of 1927, Artaud began to write to Dulac, making insistent demands on her that he should be allowed to collaborate fully on the project, and to edit the film himself. He also wanted to act the part of the clergyman in the production. He was making his living as a cinema actor at the time, appearing in both mainstream and experimental productions, and currently had a role in the Danish director Carl Dreyer's film **The Passion Of Joan Of Arc**, which was being shot in Paris. He persuaded Dreyer to release him from work for the period from 8 to 20 July, in the hope that he could prevail upon Dulac to let him act during those days in **The Seashell And The Clergyman**. Dulac, who clearly had no intention of allowing her directorial independence to be sabotaged by sharing her decisions with Artaud, then

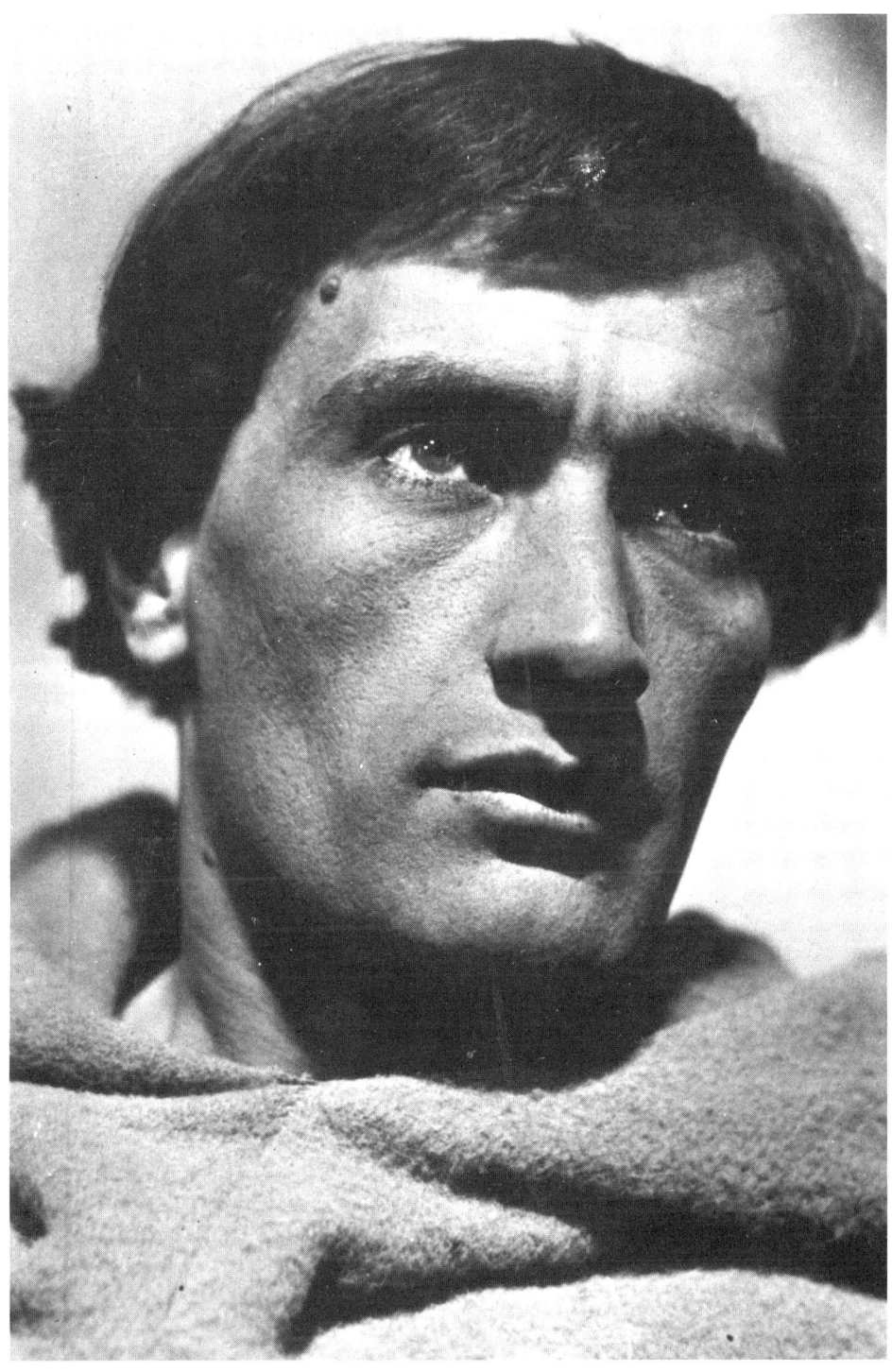

Artaud in *The Passion Of Joan Of Arc*

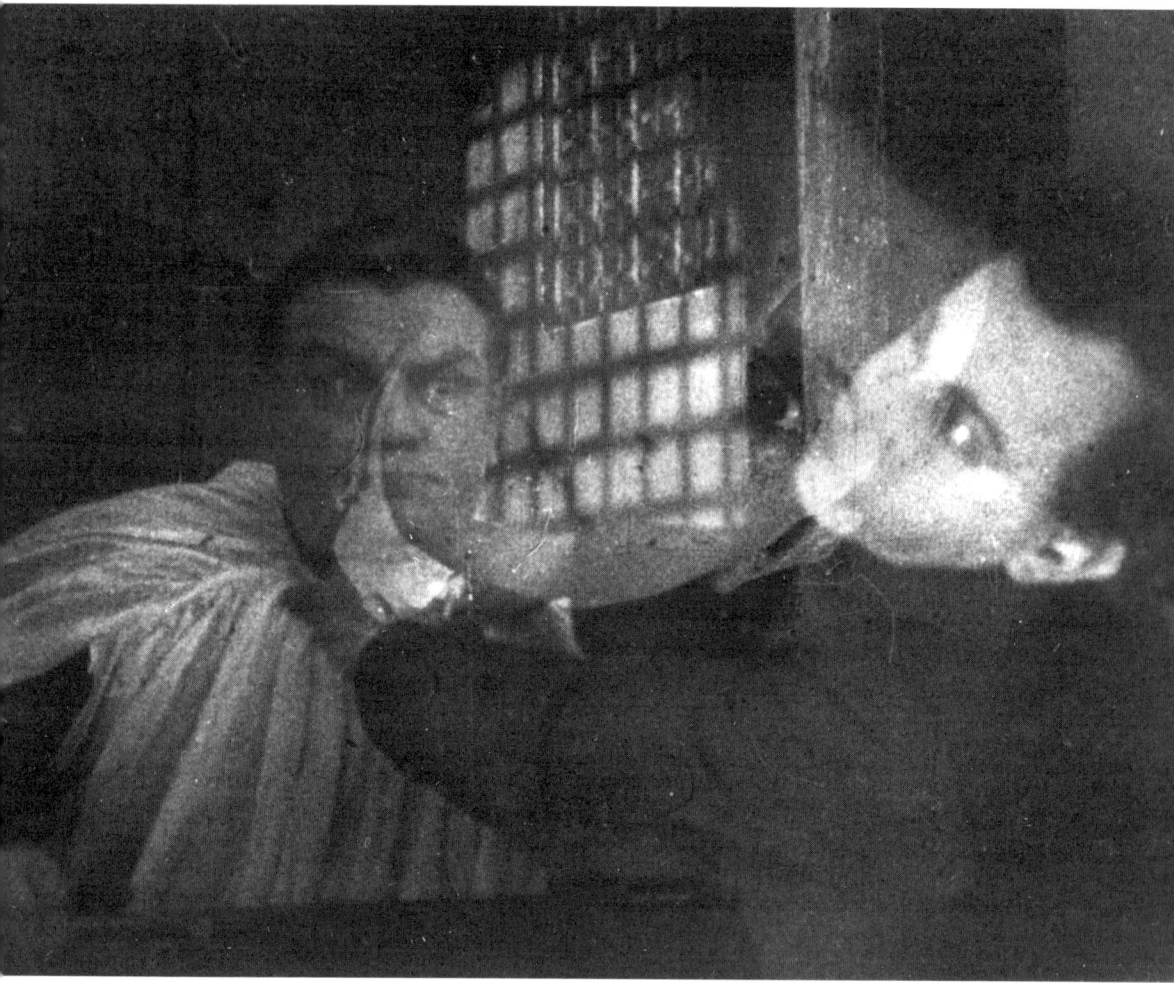

The Seashell And The Clergyman

delayed the shooting of the film and the editing sessions until August and September 1927, when Artaud was once again fully occupied with his work for Dreyer. Artaud grew increasingly angry, and when the film was screened for the first time, at the Ursulines cinema in Paris on 9 February 1928, he announced that his scenario had suffered unacceptable distortion by Dulac, who, he claimed, had "butchered" it. Despite his forcible severance from the Surrealist movement, Artaud managed to gain the alliance of a number of Surrealists (and fellow expelled Surrealists) in his protests against Dulac; the Surrealists viewed Dulac as an opportunistic interloper on their preoccupations. The Ursulines screening descended into a cultural riot of the kind which the Surrealists habitually staged throughout the 1920s. At the screening, the writer Robert Desnos initiated a volley of invective and screams directed at Germaine Dulac, and the film projection was abandoned in chaos. Two newspaper accounts gave contradictory accounts of Artaud's own participation in the brawl: in one, Artaud ran wild and shattered the cinema's hall mirrors, crying "Goulou! Goulou!"; in the other version, he was sitting quietly in the cinema with his mother, and uttered only one word during the glossolaliac uproar: "Enough".[2]

Although Artaud claimed that a manipulative disparity had been opened up by Dulac between the language of his scenario and the imagery of her film, it can be established that Dulac attempted to follow Artaud's scenario with great fidelity.[3] Her changes to the scenario are limited to practical, technical measures that enable the explicit representation of often semi-abstract images. In Artaud's original scenario, a clergyman undertakes a sequence of violent and obsessive actions. The fragmented narrative propels the clergyman through a perpetually shifting space of long corridors, crystalline landscapes and narrow city streets. He is sexually tormented in a confessional box by a beautiful woman with white hair, and vents his fury upon the figure of a lecherous military officer. The clergyman's identity collides with that of the officer, and he is constantly surrounded by shattering glass and flowing liquids. His multiple confrontations with the beautiful woman end with her suffering grotesque physical and facial distortions, her tongue "stretching out to infinity".

Dulac filmed the images of the scenario with scrupulousness, but, for Artaud, neutralized their virulence by treating them as being simply the representation of a dream. At the beginning of the film, she used the title: *The Seashell And The Clergyman: A Dream*, and gave press interviews in which she announced that she was attempting to find a filmic equivalent for a dream. This infuriated Artaud, who had an intricate theoretical concern with the workings of dream images. He objected also to the way in which the film had sutured together the raw and disjunctive images of his scenario, so that the film flowed easily for the spectator, despite the illogicality of its narrative. Dulac, who was – for that period – a technologically highly

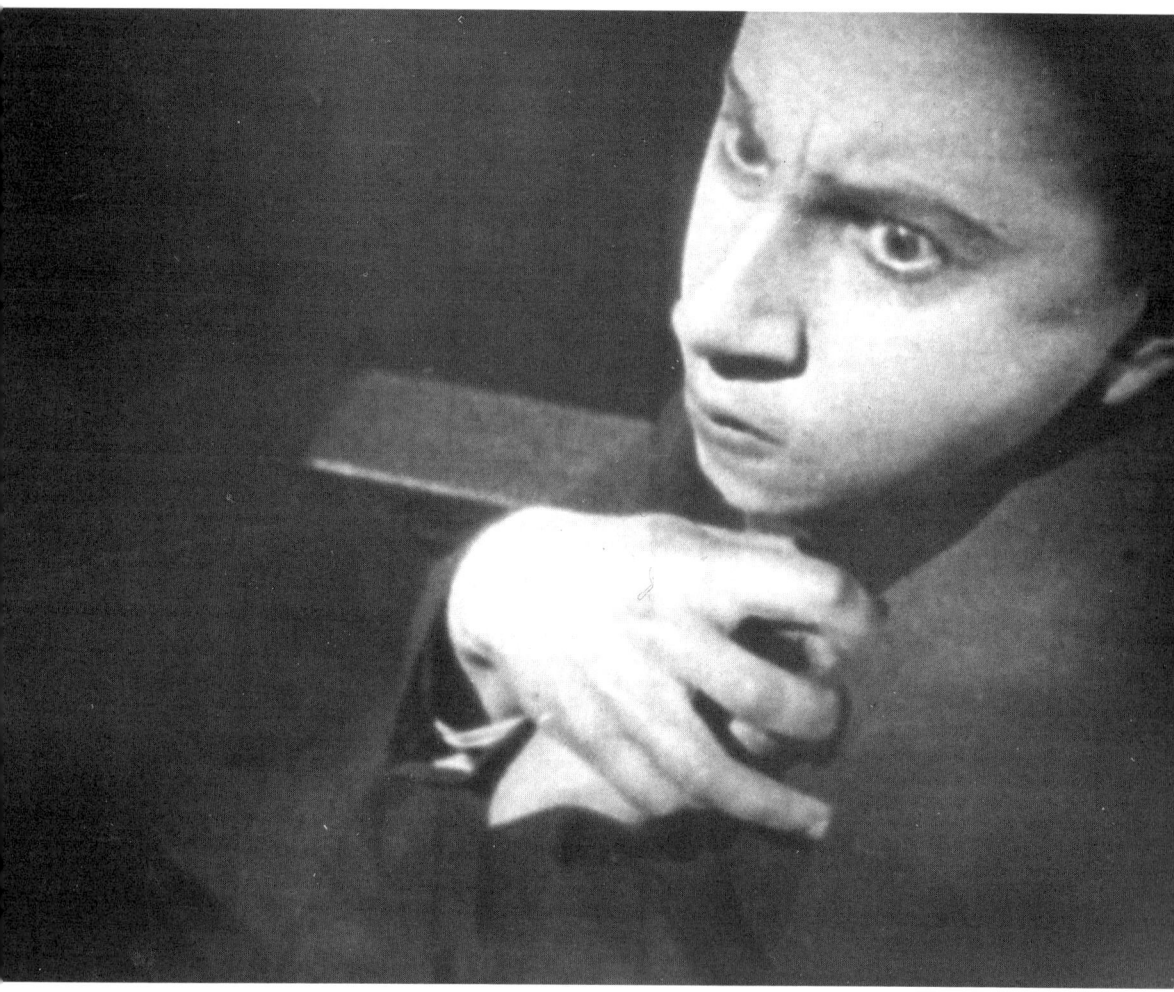

The Seashell And The Clergyman

advanced director able to execute complex superimpositions of image over image, had used every technical means at her disposal to find cinematic equivalents for Artaud's written images in his scenario, which often gave no indication of the ways in which they should be transposed into cinematic images. It was this very slavishness of Dulac's in following his work which ultimately exasperated Artaud – by duplicating his work, she had distorted and betrayed it – coupled with his anger at being excluded from the film-making process.

As a result of the riot at its première, **The Seashell And The**

Clergyman was abruptly taken off the Ursulines programme. The following year, 1929, the film's fragile reputation was entirely overshadowed by Buñuel's celebrated collaboration with Salvador Dali, **Un Chien Andalou**, which gained the prestige of being the seminal Surrealist film. Buñuel had attended the screening of **The Seashell And The Clergyman** while preparing his own film, and Artaud would claim, three years later, that **Un Chien Andalou**, along with Jean Cocteau's 1930 film **The Blood Of A Poet**, had stolen elements of the hallucinatory imagery, and the strategy of using sudden transitions of time and space, from the film whose scenario he had written. By that time, 1932, Artaud had largely reversed his negative attitude towards **The Seashell And The Clergyman**, claiming it to be a precursor of Buñuel and Cocteau's films. But despite this belated recuperation of the film on Artaud's part, and the objective resemblance between Artaud's written evocation of acts and images in his scenario and their transposition by Dulac into corresponding filmic images, a theoretical abyss separates the scenario and the film. This abyss took the form of Artaud's project for a cinema with far-reaching aims and conception. It was a cinema backed by a theory intended both to exact a radical obliteration of all cinematic history up until that point, and to create a reinvention of spectatorship, by negating the basis of film in the rapport between illusory and pacifying patterns of light and their incorporated, enmeshed spectator.

With the exception of Artaud's ideas, no theory of cinema whatsoever existed among the writers associated with the Surrealist movement at the time. There was, however, a great engagement with cinema in the Surrealist movement, and an enthusiasm for attending numerous film screenings in rapid succession in order to induce a kind of visual delirium or overload in the spectator. With the encouragement of their leader, André Breton, a number of the Surrealists were preoccupied with film as a fertile terrain of psychological investigation; Breton himself envisaged the eventual creation of a world-wide Surrealist cinema with the potential to metamorphose all perception of reality. Several Surrealists, notably Robert Desnos and Benjamin Péret, had written unfilmed scenarios in the form of descriptions of their dreams. But, in direct opposition to such descriptive work, Artaud was proposing an investigation of the systems of dreaming, with the aim of discovering their mechanisms and their collapsing structures (for Artaud, a dream always collapsed into violence and fragmentation). In this way, he intended to formulate films which would reconstitute the violent power of dreaming as a process directly projected into cinematic imagery. This would overrule interpretation or explanation: his stated aim was to "realize this idea of visual cinema where psychology itself is devoured by the acts".[4] Artaud had drawn the images for **The Seashell And The Clergyman** not from one of his own dreams, but from the transcription of a dream written down by his friend Yvonne Allendy; he viewed this distance as imperative for him to launch his attempt to seize what he saw as the visceral emanation of the process of dreaming.

Among the Surrealists, only Buñuel was able to find the finance for a sequence of films (he borrowed money from his mother and, for a time, had a wealthy patron). Artaud negatively associated Buñuel's work with the Surrealist practice of automatic writing, which he detested as creatively passive and antithetical to his own concerns with intentionality and a revolutionary struggle that was to be essentially waged around the human body. But, like Artaud (who was envisaging projects that would document cataclysmic human and natural events), Buñuel was drawn by the documentary form, and included a documentary sequence in **L'Age d'Or**. Before the financial constraints of the new sound cinema at the beginning of the 1930s terminated his film-making activities for nearly twenty years, Buñuel would make the sardonic documentary **Land Without Bread** (1932), about what he perceived to be the ignorantly self-inflicted poverty of an isolated Spanish community who threw away food and medicines because they failed to understand their uses. But Buñuel's cinema was avowedly non-theoretical: it engaged to some extent with issues of psychoanalysis, but took its own creativity as enforcing a wilful blindness towards any system of thought, however revolutionary or deviant that system might be.

Artaud developed his theory of cinema around the many other scenarios which he was writing at the time of **The Seashell And The Clergyman**. His theory of cinema appears at the intersection between the images of the scenarios and the preoccupations in language which impelled them. And to some extent, his theory of cinema emerges in direct tension with many of these scenarios. The subject matters of Artaud's scenarios – some of which were clearly written at great speed – vary very widely, and in style they range from oblique chains of unconnected images to highly accessible and cogent plot descriptions of characters engaged in physical struggles. One reason for this latter quality of accessibility in some of Artaud's scenarios was that he was always extremely short of money in the 1920s and 1930s; his theoretical concerns often clash incongruously with the need for his ideas about cinema to help to generate an income for him. For example, one of his scenarios, entitled *Flights*, was an entirely commercial project intended to connect into the increasing popular interest of the time in long-distance aviation, reflected in extensive media coverage. The plot revolves around two competing attempts to accomplish a long and difficult journey, with the protagonists affiliated to the mutually exclusive qualities of "romance" and "villainy" that prevailed in the commercial cinema of the time; after numerous trials, Artaud's romantic heroes win the aviation race in triumph. Artaud was also prepared with his scenarios to plagiarize cinema genres without compunction, and he attempted to interest the German Expressionist cinema and its offshoots in Hollywood with a horror film scenario he had written, *The 32*, which closely resembled work on the theme of the mass-murdering vampire by directors such as F. W. Murnau. As with *Flights*, *The 32* has an upbeat ending, with the vampire redeemed and society saved from further destruction. Artaud sent another of his horror film projects, *The Monk*, to the founder of the Italian Futurist art movement, F. T. Marinetti, who by this time had become an official poet of Mussolini's fascist régime and an influential figure in mainstream Italian cinema. (Artaud's project, and his request to be employed to direct films in Italy, were ignored by Marinetti.) Many of Artaud's commercial scenarios of the second half of the 1920s give the impression of a futile attempt to ingratiate himself with the formulaic mainstream film culture of the time, though each of them also contains an intermittently startling imagery of the body in extreme crisis. *The Seashell And The Clergyman* was the third of Artaud's scenarios, which number fifteen in all. By far the most extraordinary of all of the scenarios is the very last one, *The Butcher's Revolt*, which Artaud again intended to direct himself and for which he drew up an intricate – though, in its mathematical calculations, completely inaccurate – budget.

The Butcher's Revolt was written early in 1930, at the crucial point of crossover between the end of silent cinema and the innovation of sound cinema. The scenario possesses a far more cohesive narrative than *The Seashell And The Clergyman*; it even takes place in a specific location, around the Place de l'Alma in Paris. The principal figure in the scenario, introduced with irony by Artaud as "the madman", is in a dangerously obsessive state. While waiting to meet a woman in the street, he watches a carcass of meat fall from a speeding butcher's truck and becomes fascinated by the rapport between the texture of the meat and that of human flesh. He immediately provokes a brawl in a nearby café, and then takes part in a sequence of headlong chases (recalling those from Hollywood silent comedy films) which culminate in his arrival at a slaughterhouse and his humiliation there at the hands of the police. As with *The Seashell And The Clergyman*, the identity of the protagonist is volatile, and he experiences extremes of sensation, from joy to paralysing despair. The action of the scenario is powered by sudden transformations of space, punctuated by occasional outbursts of words, screams and noises.

In all of his scenarios before *The Butcher's Revolt*, Artaud had conveyed an adamant opposition to the introduction of sound into his film work. This was the moment of heated debate throughout Europe about whether the new technology of sound in cinema should be resisted or welcomed. In a lecture which he had delivered on 29 June 1929 at a cinema specializing in experimental work, the Studio 28 in Montmartre, Artaud declared: "There is no possible identification between sound and image. The image presents itself only in one dimension – it's the translation, the transposition of the real; sound, on the contrary, is unique and true, it bursts out into the room, and acts by consequence with much more intensity than the image, which becomes only a kind of illusion of sound."[5] Sound, for Artaud, would have to be separated from the image, in order for the image to maintain its own, autonomous resonances and impact. But the following year, with *The Butcher's Revolt*, Artaud attempted to come to terms with the growing inter-relationship of sound and image in cinema; he now viewed the element of mutual destructiveness which he perceived within this relationship as potentially valuable to his aims. He allowed a number of isolated and obsessive phrases (such as: "I've had enough of cutting up meat without eating it") into his scenario, typographically emphasizing them and enclosing them in black-bordered boxes. The words served as a way of imparting an abrupt emphasis to the visual imagery, which would, he believed, rebound from the image/sound collision with greater ferocity. The tense interaction of image, word and sound extended to Artaud's presentation of the scenario's content and its implications for spectatorship. In a note preceding the publication in June 1930 of his scenario in the literary periodical *La Nouvelle Revue Française*, Artaud summarised the content of the imagery: "eroticism, cruelty, the taste for blood, the search for violence, obsession with the horrible, dissolution of moral values, social hypocrisy, lies, false witness, sadism, perversity..." – all of this would be made explicitly visible for the spectator with "the maximum readability".[6] The vision of horror would itself become a visceral but disciplined language.

Artaud's strategy for sound in *The Butcher's Revolt* prefigures that used in his recording for radio, *To Have Done With The Judgement Of God*, eighteen years later. There, the sound effects – screams and rhythmic, percussive beatings – became inserted into Artaud's recited language of expulsion and refusal, with an immediate incision. In the recording, the violent physical gesture of the scream cuts across the escalating rush of the language's imagery in the way that, in Artaud's plan for *The Butcher's Revolt*, noise would have vitally lacerated the flow of the visual images. Similarly, in Artaud's notebook drawings of the mid-1940s, the entangled arrangements of texts and images are often seared by a sudden gesture of obliteration – a pencil stroke that abruptly makes its trajectory across the page, simultaneously reinforcing the powerful visual emanation of language and image as it cancels them.

In *The Butcher's Revolt*, the primacy accorded by Artaud to the image and its spatial presence broke with the predominant film style of the time, which consisted of a kind of filmed theatre that emphasized psychological dialogue and the passage of time. In his note about *The Butcher's Revolt*, Artaud stressed the spatial quality of the reinforced sound which he would employ: "The voices are in space, like objects."[7] Space is a crucial element in Artaud's conception of film. There is a constant preoccupation with expanding and manipulating the spatial dimension while erasing or reducing time. The passage from film frame to frame is an especial danger in Artaud's perception; each image must be emphasised to such intensity that the intervening passage of time between the images can be suppressed to its maximum degree. In his "Theatre of Cruelty" of the early 1930s, there is a parallel concern with spatial movement: the actor's gesture must burn itself out into space with unique immediacy and impact, and must not be repeated in time. The very first of Artaud's film scenarios, *Eighteen Seconds*, from 1924, evokes the thoughts of an actor during the period of eighteen seconds between the moment at which he looks at his watch and the moment at which he shoots himself in the street. A complex sequence of images and spatial mutations is arranged into a condensed period of time, which would then have to be expanded to an hour or two of cinematic duration. Since the process of representation operates for Artaud on a temporal level, on which sound and image are repeated and disseminated, his determination to introduce a spatial rather than temporal element into film sound signalled a denial of the movement towards diminishment and repetition which any completed, represented art object makes. In Artaud's conception of cinema, the presence of the human body in which the film has its axis must be immediate and dense. It is likely that Artaud was aware of a precedent to this aspect of his theory, in the form of the Italian Futurist film manifesto of November 1916, which had demanded "polyexpressiveness" and proposed "filmed unreal reconstructions of the human body".[8] With a scenario such as *The Butcher's Revolt* that projected the amalgamation of diverse, volatile physical elements into a spatially flexible and eruptive structure, Artaud was envisaging a cinema which – like all of his subsequent visual and aural work – was acutely resistant to representation.

Despite prolonged efforts, Artaud failed to find the money to finance the planned production of *The Butcher's Revolt*. He abandoned writing scenarios and his theoretical work on the cinema tailed off at the same time, while, for the next five years, he was forced to continue acting in films – an occupation which he viewed as menial and humiliating. His film-acting

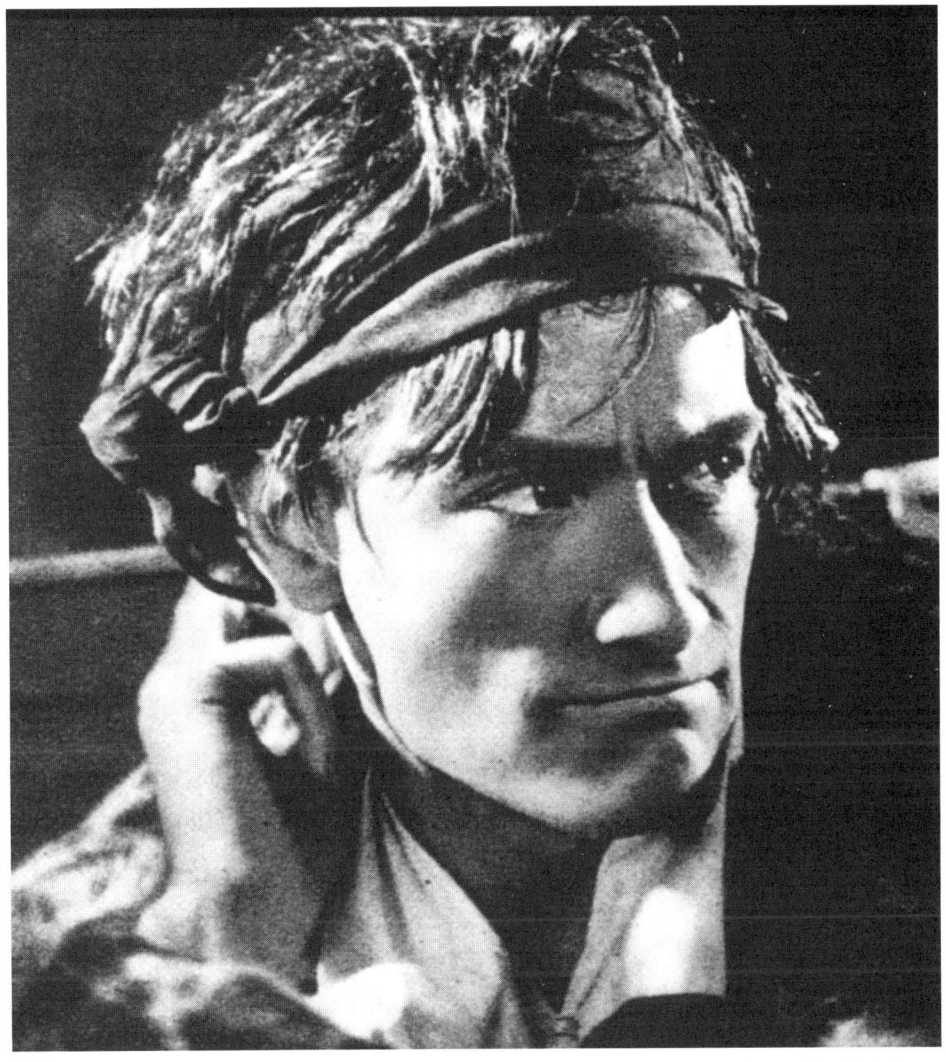

Artaud in *Napoleon*

career had started well, with his part in the director Claude Autant-Lara's experimental first film **Fait Divers**[9], produced in 1924, the same year as Artaud also wrote his own first film scenario. For a time in the second half of the 1920s, Artaud was well on his way to becoming a film star.[10] He made twenty-two film-acting appearances in all, from 1924 to 1935. Among the most successful of these were his startling presences in Jean Painlevé's **Mathusalem**, in Abel Gance's **Napoleon** (he appeared both in the silent

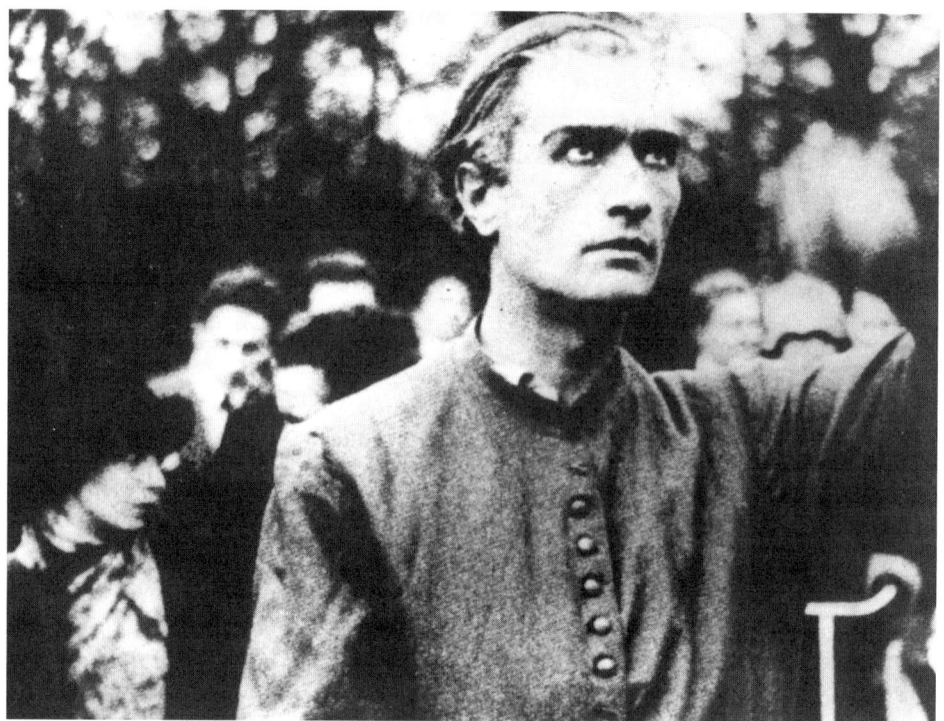

Artaud in *Mathusalem*

version of 1926 and the sound version of 1935), in Carl Dreyer's 1927 film **The Passion Of Joan Of Arc** – the film whose shooting had coincided with that of **The Seashell And The Clergyman** – and in Fritz Lang's only French film, **Liliom**, from 1933. His unusual acting in all of these films oscillates with gestural control between paroxysmal facial seizures and a kind of broken emotional grandeur. Artaud also travelled to Berlin three times (twice in 1930 and once in 1932) to act in films for the German cinema industry. He had a small role in G. W. Pabst's film of Bertolt Brecht's **The Threepenny Opera**, a film which Artaud despised for what he called its "vulgarity and its complete *disorientation*".[11] In fact, almost all of these films – with the exception of his work for Dreyer – constituted painfully degrading work for Artaud, most especially Raymond Bernard's abysmal epic of patriotic fervour, **The Wooden Crosses**, from 1931, in which Artaud plays an enthusiastic French soldier in the First World War who leaps over the edge of the trench towards the Germans, yelling: "I shit on you, you bastards!"

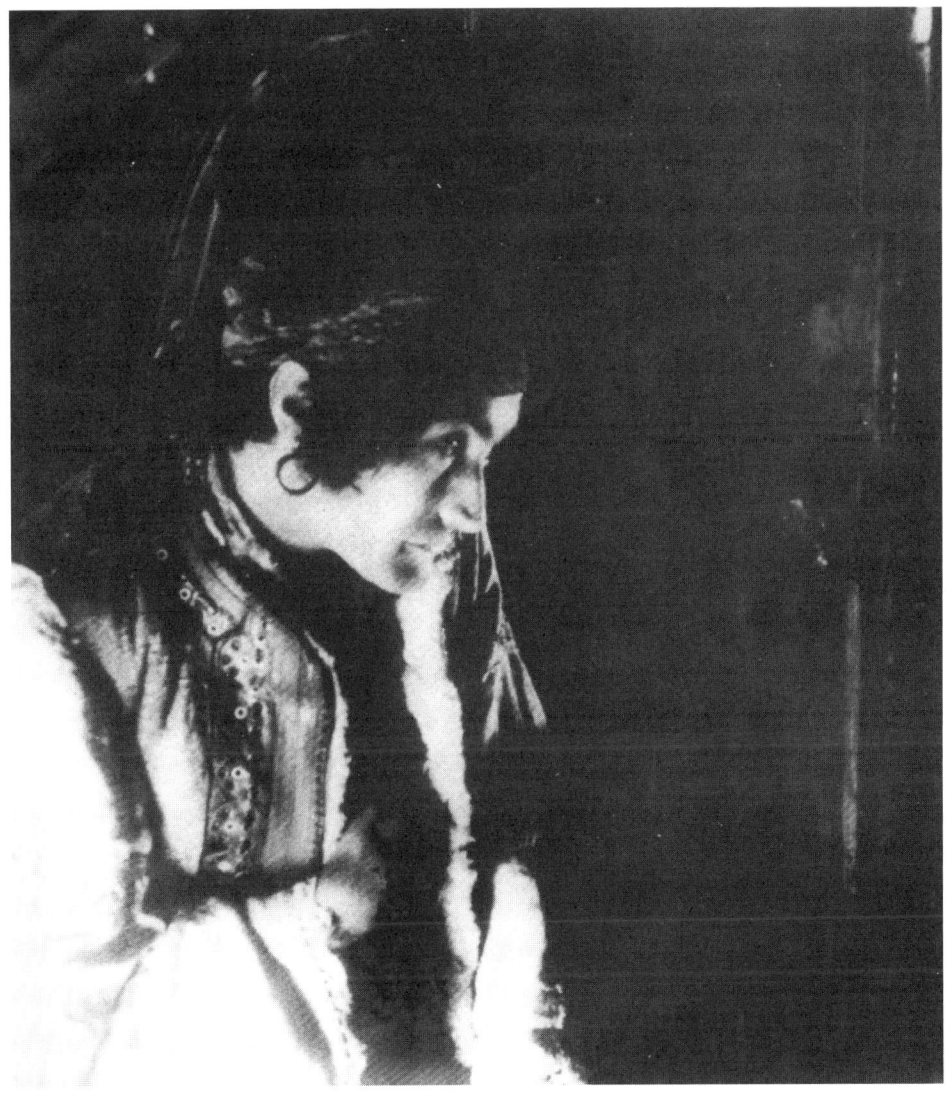

Artaud in *Tarakanova*

(Artaud had also appeared in Bernard's **Tarakanova** of 1929). This "abominable work"[12], as he called it, contributed to the exhaustion of Artaud's engagement with cinema of every kind, and in 1932 he would conclude: "I am ever more convinced that the cinema is and will remain the art of the past. You cannot work in it without feeling ashamed."[13]

    An innovative and extreme theory of cinema emerges from the short series of texts which Artaud produced at the same time as writing his scenarios. Artaud's theory of cinema is a theory of fragments. It is an oblique, tangential theory with an impulse towards self-cancellation. To some extent, Artaud's theory of cinema serves directly to disassemble and negate the practical attempts which he was making simultaneously to create film works.

Artaud's theoretical film writing, like all of his work, exists in a state of constant flux, with points of abandonment followed by points of resurgence. Artaud writes with the greatest degree of vision and theoretical acuity about film projects which he has already definitively abandoned. His proposals for the cinema are often best seized, in their ephemerality, on the margin of overlap between his theoretical texts and the letters he wrote about his theories, to figures such as the magazine editor Jean Paulhan. The form of the letter was always a privileged site for Artaud in the dissemination of his theoretical work – a form in which polemical exhortation could be allied to direct address. For Artaud, the letter had the effect of imparting confidential or urgent information in the form of a kind of written contract; once the addressee had received the letter, they were involuntarily and compulsorily bound into Artaud's project as a supporter. In Artaud's acutely heterogeneous "letters of theory", as they might be called, the content oscillates wildly between individual obsession and an objective interrogation of wider subject matters, such as the origins and processes of dreaming. In exploring the potential of Artaud's theory of cinema, then, what needs to be pinpointed is the space of intersection between his avowedly theoretical fragments, his letters of theory, and the scenarios that sought visually to form a counterpart – simultaneously interlinked and deeply divisive – to his linguistic preoccupations with the cinema. A final element in this conglomeration of material is Dulac's **The Seashell And The Clergyman**, with its superficial but loyal attachment to Artaud's images.

In Artaud's theory of cinema, representation is perceived as an abyss. From his earliest writings, such as his correspondence with Jacques Rivière on the nature of poetry, Artaud had spoken of a dual trap, within which all of his attempts to create language fell apart. Firstly, he was faced with the dispersal of his language through inarticulation – the intractable slippages which his mental images suffered as they were brought into a textual form.

And secondly, on the occasions when he was finally able to assemble a text, he was immediately faced with its loss into representation, which he perceived as the stealing-away of the unique or original relevance which his language had possessed to his physical presence. In Artaud's work, the body is everything: to transform or transmit the body is the intention of all his work. His incessant hostility towards the process of representation – as the power which assimilates and sabotages this intention – endured throughout his work, and would become most angrily forceful in his approach to his drawings and recordings of 1946–48. By the time he came to work on his final project, *To Have Done With The Judgement Of God*, Artaud would conceive of representation as being inextricably and maliciously linked to social and religious institutions, writing in 1947: "there is nothing I abominate and execrate so much as this idea... of representation,/that is, of virtuality, of non-reality... attached to all that is produced and shown, as if it were intended in that way to socialize and at the same time paralyse monsters, to make the possibilities of explosive deflagration which are too dangerous for life pass instead by the channel of the stage, screen or microphone, and so turn them away from life."[14] Artaud's theory of cinema is one of the primary points of origin for this unique rage against representation, since the essential focus of his rage at this time is the gap of representation between language and image. That gap is what impairs the transmission of his imageries of the human body. For Artaud, the arena of cinema is made up of intangible plays of light, of temporal delays and spatial wastelands, all of which constitute the dead zone of representation.[15] Representation works to deny his conception of a filmic work in direct contact with the human body; the image is always stripped of its imminence. But, at the time of his film work (in contrast to his later work in drawings and recordings), Artaud still recognized that the element of mediation is inescapable in the cinema, and that it had to be both ambushed and worked with. His film theory, then, formulates a confrontation with representation, with the aim of tearing the image away from representation, to transplant it directly into the film spectator's ocular nerves and sensations.

Artaud aimed to make his film images dense – and so resistant to the temporal process of representation – by emphasizing their existence in space

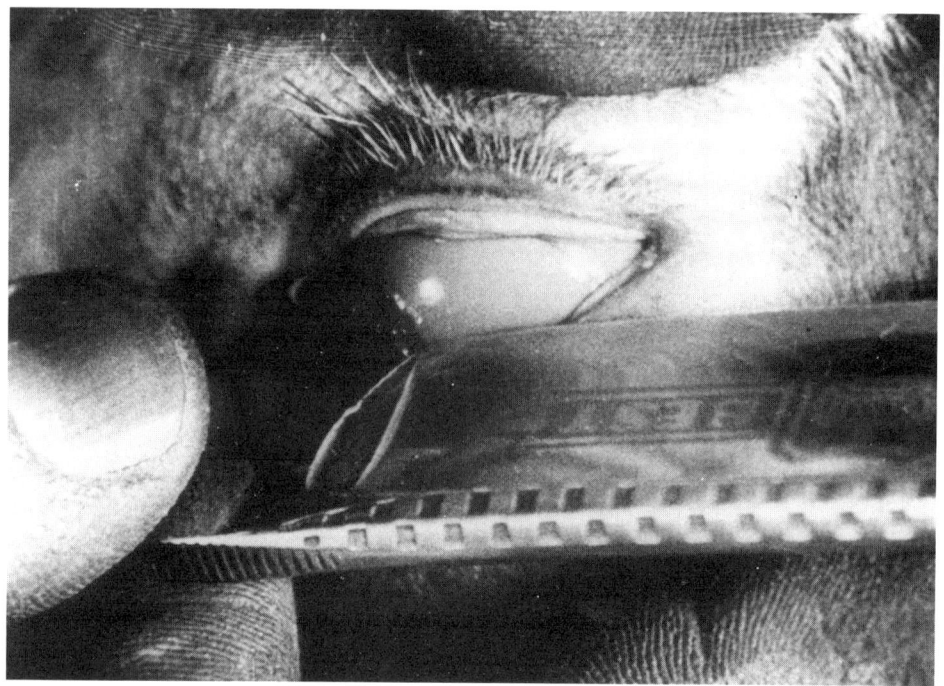

Ocular destruction: *Un Chien Andalou*

and their sense of perpetual movement. Around these images of the body, all of the other elements in his scenarios are articulated only to the extent that they are then immediately suppressed, destroyed or subtracted from his filmic world. His film language becomes one of dissolution, with an arrhythmic narrative, and with images pounded down to compact visual sensation. He wrote: "search for a film with purely visual sensations in which the force would emerge from a collision exacted on the eyes".[16] (The constant emphasis on an ocular attack upon the spectator in Artaud's film work necessarily recalls the literal eye-slitting, with its own implications for spectatorship, which is staged at the opening of Buñuel's **Un Chien Andalou** – a film that, as noted earlier, the director was preparing at the time he saw **The Seashell And The Clergyman**.) For Artaud, the concentrated impact which his film would exert on its spectator's perception would result from the disjunctive but accumulating force of his images, amassing to produce a dynamic and essentially spatial inscription of his concerns. With a project such as *The Butcher's Revolt*, the imagery's sensory charge would be accentuated still further by its juxtaposition with elements of noise and with verbal outbursts.

Artaud's conception of cinema moves away from the dominant film fiction of the time – with its attempt to invisibly integrate the new sound technology with the image – towards a more jarring interaction of elements of control and chance. In inviting a disruptive element of chance into his otherwise rigorously formulated work, Artaud was engaging to some degree with the documentary film form, in which directorial intention was ostensibly always subject to being over-ruled by the random emanation and perverse occurrences of reality itself.[17] All of Artaud's scenarios project an atmosphere of darkness, blood and shock at the boundary between intention and chance. This is the point where opposites meet and collide – divisions between reality and fiction, and between the individual and an engulfing society. Artaud's film theory delineates a conflict staged upon borderlines, spatially charting the trajectories of what he calls "the simple impact of objects, forms, repulsions, attractions".[18] The borders of image and language inhabited by Artaud's film work are the sites of these multiple collisions, most notably between the subjective and social realities which he would later interrogate in his recorded work. His obstinate traversal of textual and visual borders always implies a negative push: the image stays in the domain of the image, or else risks annihilation. In this relentless collapsing of borders, Artaud's film theory moves towards a fall into catastrophe – in fact, towards a zone in which the filmic counterpart to the theory is desired but impossible. And in this theory, the image aimed for and the spectator aimed at would be in a dangerous state of interaction.

Artaud's film theory intends to force its spectators into a position of subjugation to its imageries, with its visual flood of disintegration and disaster; but, at the same time, the theory espouses a violent unleashing of the spectators' senses – those spectators remain alertly grounded in the tactile world, aware both of what the film is subjecting them to, and also incited to react, in simultaneously physical and revolutionary ways. Artaud's theoretical writings and his scenarios possess and maintain their own relentlessly self-annihilating logic which is never transgressed, and moves toward the act of demonstrating images of the insurgent human body at their most stripped-away and condensed – and thereby, in Artaud's conception, at their most resistant to the process of representation. His scenarios are expelled under great internal pressure from his obsessions, and are pitched to explode in the spectator's eyes – directly conveying "the convulsions and jumps of a reality which seems to destroy itself with an irony where you can hear the extremities of the mind screaming."[19]

For Artaud, the cinema was literally a stimulant or narcotic, acting directly and materially on the eyes and the senses. He called his film projects "raw cinema"[20], and though they were designed initially to investigate the mechanisms of dreaming, they came to demand a more immediately physical contact between the cinematic image and the spectator. Like Artaud's "Theatre of Cruelty" of the mid-1930s, this was a language of film that could work only once – taking the form of one unique film and, in theory, one sole and unrepeatable screening and one set of spectators. It avoided to its extreme limit the process of signification and representation, using instead an imagery compacted together from control, chance and the body's projection.

Artaud's project for the cinema is, in historical terms, lost. It aimed to divert the future course of cinema (and to cancel out cinema's pre-existing course) at a moment of great transformation – that of the coming of sound – when it appeared possible that film could be sent into an unknown direction with the potential for a new relationship between the film and its audience. Many other extraordinary experiments and theories of cinema were being formulated at the same time as Artaud's plans. In the Soviet Union, Dziga Vertov's polemics about spectatorship and revolution were, in their way, as visionary and radical as Artaud's. But, where Vertov was able to direct his film **The Man With The Movie Camera**, Artaud produced nothing. Artaud's vision of cinema, not least because of its integral self-cancellation, cannot stand on the strength of its celluloid imagery (which goes no further than the first, directionless step of **The Seashell And The Clergyman**). Where Buñuel's films gained an aura of enigma through the consistent theoretical reticence of their maker, Artaud's cinema is all theory and written images, and no films. Like his drawings of the mid-1940s, it is in raging flux

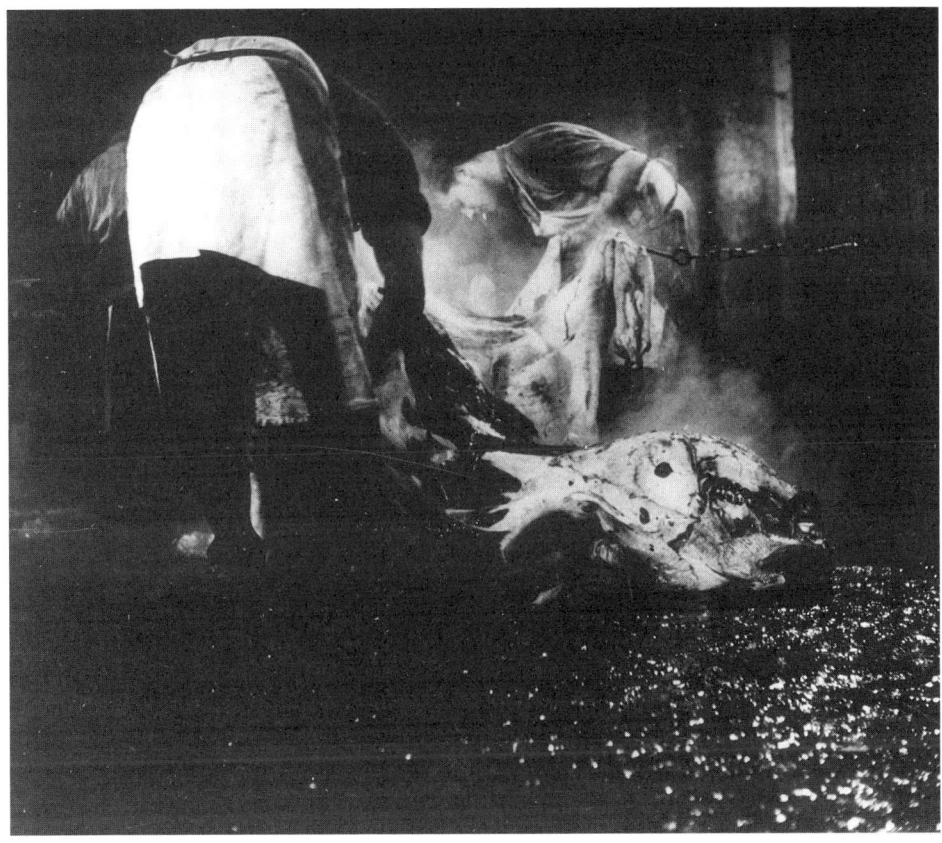

Georges Franju's *The Blood Of The Beasts*

between imagery and commentary. As the history of cinema transpired, the meshing together of sound and image which Artaud had protested against in 1929 also effectively terminated the first headlong rush of Buñuel's cinema, and brought to an end the great experimental decade of European cinema.

Artaud's cinema has only one direct successor: the Lettrist cinema of the early 1950s created by Isidore Isou and Maurice Lemaître, with its emphasis on negation and its violent approach to spectatorship.[21] A scattering of other films have taken on elements of Artaud's project for cinema. Georges Franju's 1949 hybrid amalgam of documentary and hallucination, **The Blood Of The Beasts** – set in the Parisian slaughter-houses, and shot in the face of palpable hostility and invective towards the film-maker from the slaughterhouse workers as they slit multiple throats with insouciance – absorbs both Artaud's concern with the documentary form, and the blood-saturated atmosphere of *The Butcher's Revolt*. The ritual films of the legendary Vienna Action Group of artists – particularly those by Otto Muehl and Hermann Nitsch, who were both strongly preoccupied with Artaud's work in the mid-1960s, when they were documenting their performances through film works – also approach the rigorous collision of blood, slaughter and chance which Artaud had envisaged for film.[22]

Artaud desired a cinema that could confront the fragmentation and the horror of representation that ran throughout his work. The spectator of his proposed cinema is placed at the very extremes of visual experience, physically exposed to a multiple criss-crossing of expulsive forces which necessitate a transformation of the conditions and nature of visual perception, and impel a resistance towards society and towards cinema itself.

NOTES

The most valuable documents on Artaud's work in cinema are those accompanying the film retrospectives held in Paris at the Centre Georges Pompidou in 1987, edited by Jean-Paul Morel, and in London at the National Film Theatre in 1993, edited by Stephen Barber and Jane Giles. All of Artaud's film scenarios and his essays on cinema – usually formulated in short, fragmentary texts of two or three pages – are included in Volume III (1978) of the *Oeuvres Complètes* (*Collected Works*), 1956–1994, published by Éditions Gallimard in Paris and edited anonymously by Paule Thévenin.

(1) **The Seashell And The Clergyman** was distributed in this version by the American company Glenn Photo Supply, which distributed 16mm film copies to Britain. It took until the early 1980s before an American film historian, Sandy Flitterman-Lewis (who was writing a book on the work of the film's director, Germaine Dulac), noticed that the reels were in the wrong order. This discovery appears not to have reached the film's distributors, unless they were oblivious to it, since they continue to use the mis-edited version.

(2) This account is drawn from a consultation of a series of manuscript letters between Artaud and Germaine Dulac, held in the library collection of the Bibliothèque de l'Arsenal in Paris, together with an archive of newspaper accounts of the Ursulines screening and statements made by Artaud and Dulac to the press about the film.

(3) The original manuscript of the scenario of **The Seashell And The Clergyman**, and Dulac's shooting script in its various stages, are in the library collection of the Bibliothèque de l'Arsenal.

(4) Antonin Artaud, *Cinéma Et Réalité* (1927), collected in *Oeuvres Complètes*, Volume III, Éditions Gallimard, Paris, 1978, page 19.

(5) Antonin Artaud, extract from lecture (1929), *Oeuvres Complètes*, Volume III, page 377.

(6) Antonin Artaud, untitled note (1930) accompanying *La Révolte Du Boucher*, in *Oeuvres Complètes*, Volume III, page 54.

(7) ibid, page 54.

(8) Film manifesto entitled "The Futurist Cinema", originally published in the journal *L'Italia Futurista*, Rome, issue 9, 11 November 1916, and reproduced in part in the catalogue *Film As Film*, Hayward Gallery, London, 1979, pages 79–80. Every one of the films made by the Italian Futurist movement in the 1910s has been lost.

(9) In **Fait Divers**, Artaud plays a suave, lipstick-wearing adulterer with sperm-stained trousers who is strangled to death by his lover's irate husband. Claude Autant-Lara was only twenty-three years old when he directed **Fait Divers**. The film's aura of compulsion and obsession, together with its intricate superimpositions and slow-motion sequences, all prefigure those in Germaine Dulac's **The Seashell And The Clergyman** (particularly the erotic scene of Artaud's slow-motion strangulation, which parallels the throttling of the lecherous military officer in Dulac's film). Autant-Lara went on to become a successful mainstream film director, but the attacks of the French "New Wave" critics on what they saw as his "archaic, bourgeois melodramas" contributed to the premature end of his film-directing career at the beginning of the 1960s; however, he began a prominent new career at the end of the 1980s, aged almost ninety, as an extreme right-wing Member of the European Parliament.

(10) When Artaud died in March 1948, long after his film-acting career was over, affectionate obituaries of him appeared in numerous French film-fan magazines.

(11) Antonin Artaud, letter to Jean Paulhan, 22 January 1932, *Oeuvres Complètes*, Volume III, page 261.

(12) Antonin Artaud, letter to Yvonne Allendy, 2 June 1931, *Oeuvres Complètes*, Volume III, page 207.

(13) Antonin Artaud, letter to Louis Jouvet, 20 May 1932, *Oeuvres Complètes*, Volume III, page 283.

(14) Antonin Artaud, working notes (November 1947) towards *Pour En Finir Avec Le Jugement De Dieu*, in *Oeuvres Complètes*, Volume XIII, 1974, pages 258–259.

(15) By way of a contrast, the celebrated French film director Robert Bresson's approach to representation is exactly the inverse of Artaud's in formulation, but is strangely similar in intention and result. Where Artaud

wants to refuse representation but project everything (that is, the body), Bresson declared that his sparse, condensed kind of cinema is "the art, with images, of representing nothing". Robert Bresson, *Notes Sur Le Cinématographie*, Éditions Gallimard, 1975, page 20.

(16) *Cinéma Et Réalité*, page 19.

(17) There are notable exceptions to this. In Luis Buñuel's documentary, **Land Without Bread**, for example, the film's voice-over describes how things are so bad and backward in the poverty-stricken Spanish village which is the subject of the film that the villagers' livestock voluntarily commit suicide by jumping over a cliff. The film shows the animals doing this. But when the image is studied closely, it's just possible to see the film crew pushing the animals over the cliff.

(18) *Cinéma Et Réalité*, page 20.

(19) ibid, page 20.

(20) Antonin Artaud, *Sorcellerie Et Cinéma* (1927), *Oeuvres Complètes*, Volume III, page 66.

(21) The Lettrists were the last, most redundant, and least known, of the great twentieth-century Parisian art movements. The Situationist movement – which played a key part in the May 1968 riots in Paris – emerged in the early 1950s as a dissident offshoot of the Lettrists, whose leader, Isidore Isou (born in Rumania in 1925), was a crazed autocrat in the mould of André Breton; many of the young writers and artists who had been associated with the group, such as Guy Debord and François Dufrêne, made an early departure from Isou's tyrannical but dishevelled movement. The best-known works of the Lettrist cinema are Isou's film **Tract Of Drool And Eternity** (*Traité De Bave Et D'Eternité*) and Maurice Lemaître's film **Has The Film Already Started?** (*Le Film Est Déjà Commencé?*), both from 1951. The Lettrist group knew Artaud's work well and they had come into personal contact with him during the last year of his life – they would often go up to Artaud and harangue him (to Artaud's total indifference) as he sat writing in cafés. Isou's two-hour-long film aims to negate both itself and the entire history of cinema up to that point. The sound and image of the film are set in confrontation with one another: Isou strategically resists the cohering and assimilating nature of film sound, as Artaud had in 1929, and subjects the

spectator to a hallucinatory accumulation of damaged images (the celluloid itself is scratched and obliterated). For Isou, the attacked spectator's sensory upheaval is in itself revolutionary. The film was a seminal influence on the work of the American experimental film-maker Stan Brakhage. Lemaître's film uses the same strategies as Isou's, but with greater ferocity. Accounts of the events surrounding the first screening of Lemaître's one-hour-long hand-coloured film particularly recall the self-destruction integral to Artaud's own film work and its corrosive approach to spectatorship. Before the film's screening, Lemaître threw rubbish at the people queuing to be admitted to the cinema. He also offered money to couples in the queue, suggesting they should use it to pay for a hotel room to have sex rather than wasting their time watching his film. During the projection of the film, Lemaître threw buckets of water at his spectators and fired off a gun; finally, he called the police and the projection ended in a riot. His strategy of negation continued even after the film's few screenings. Lemaître left the original negative of the film for over forty years in a damp corner, hoping that it would deteriorate to the point where it could no longer be projected. Finally though, in 1993, he decided that his film was now a historical document and restored it – newly hand-colouring the negative – before it was released in video format by Light Cone Video, Paris, in 1995.

(22) The Vienna Action Group's crucial work took place in the mid-1960s when the young artists Günter Brus, Hermann Nitsch and Otto Muehl, all of whom allied their work closely with that of Artaud, staged performances which explored the vulnerability of the human body to obliteration. Their obsession took the form of highly disciplined rituals of sacrifice and horror, performed in public, in which they would cut open the carcasses of animals over the naked bodies of the performers, so that the spilled organs of the animals became indistinguishable from the human sexual organs. The performance space was drenched in blood. The performances were documented by handheld 8mm and 16mm film cameras; the volatile, out-of-control quality of the resulting black-and-white films was generated by the inability of the wildly moving cameras to document more than chance elements of the spectacles, which possess a vertiginous impact of carnage on film. The work of the other major participant of the Action Group, Rudolph

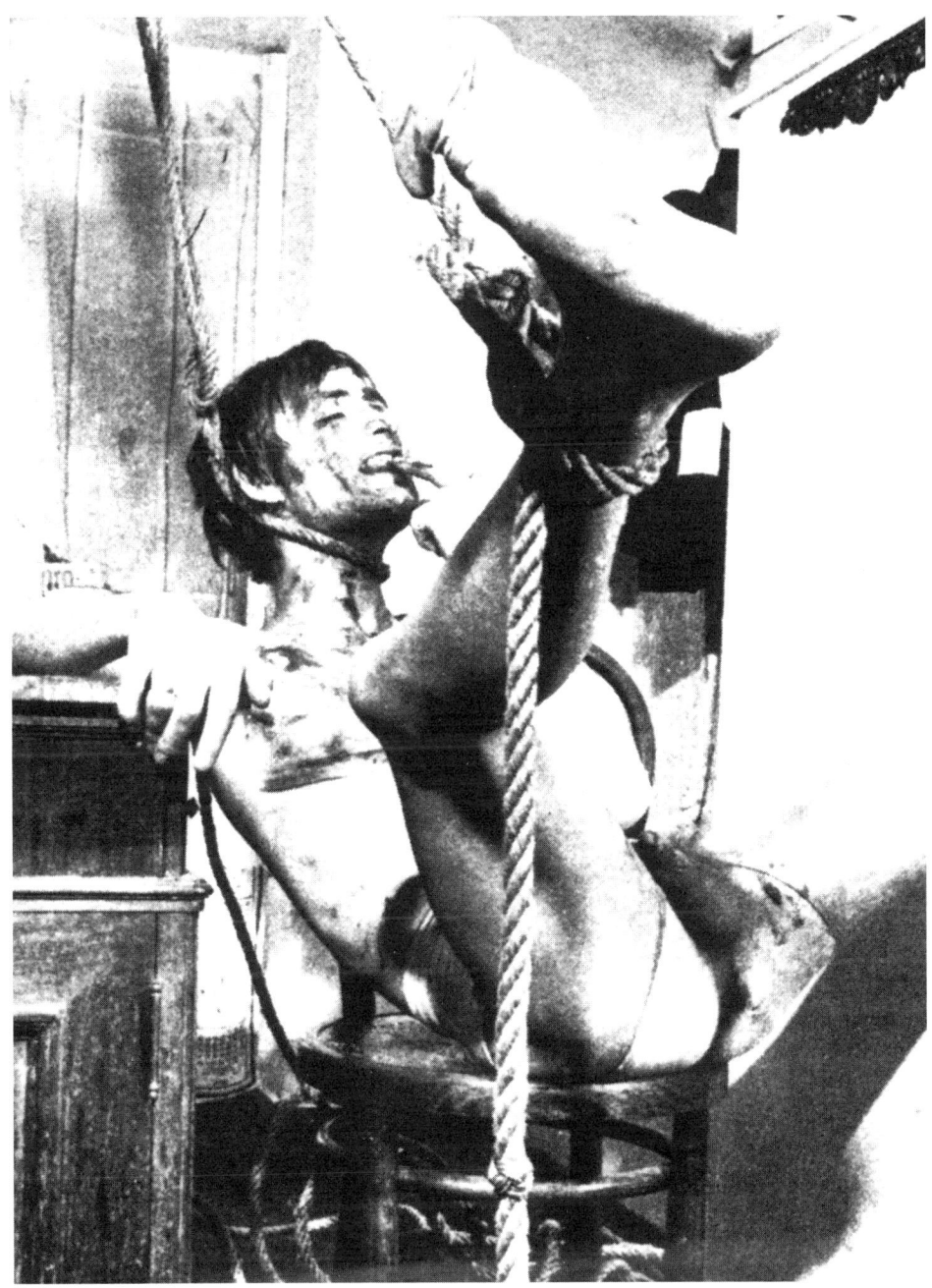

Günter Brus in Action Group performance, 1968

Schwarzkogler, was privately documented by photography rather than film, and inhabited a zone of acute exposure and isolation; his performers had

33

razor blades attached to their penises while their hands were bandaged, and their mouths gagged and stuffed with wire. The work of the Action Group was driven by their derision for the fascism which they viewed as being still tangible in the everyday life of their city – the Austrian social bureaucracy, active in the Nazis' management of wartime genocide and oppression, had survived and needed to be attacked. The Action Group was also intent on producing images of human existence under the impact of a meticulously created violence, which would erupt in performance in virulent sprays and gestures of blood. Their performances proved acutely provocative, even within the context of the 1960s; the artists were incessantly arrested and Schwarzkogler, after abandoning his performance work in dejection, committed suicide in 1969 by throwing himself from the window of his apartment. Both Nitsch and Muehl attempted to create oppositional communities to negate the society they despised. Nitsch bought the derelict Prinzendorf castle in rural Austria and established a commune of artists (still in existence) who staged and filmed Artaud-inspired ritual performances of bloodshed, meat and screams with cathartic aims. Muehl's community was more corrosive and extreme than that of Nitsch, whose work became lauded even by the Austrian government in the 1990s. Muehl founded his nihilistic, sexually-charged "AA Kommune" in which the idea of ownership was outlawed, but his experiment ended in calamity when the commune perversely evolved from its original aim of revolutionary equality into total dictatorship (with Muehl in the position of abusive power); Muehl spent much of the 1990s in prison after being convicted for having sex with children in the commune. Films of the Vienna Action Group can be viewed, along with films by artists associated with them (notably Kurt Kren and Ernst Schmidt), at events such as exhibitions of work by Nitsch. (Interviews with Hermann Nitsch and Ursula Krinzinger, Vienna, February 1992.) For further information, see *The Art Of Destruction: The Films of The Vienna Action Group* by Stephen Barber (Creation Books, 2004).

Appendix One

"The Butcher's Revolt"
(Antonin Artaud, 1930)

The Seashell and the Clergyman is the first film of subjective images – not tinged with humour – ever to have been written and directed. Other films, before that one, had introduced into the mind a similar rupture of logic – but their sense of being *unleashed* always had its clearest explanation, and its reason for existing, in humour.

The workings of this genre of films – even when applied to serious subject matters – replicate something very similar to the workings of laughter. Humour is the common denominator here, experienced by everybody: it is the medium by which the mind communicates to us its secrets.

The Seashell and the Clergyman is the first-ever film of a subjective kind where an attempt was made to confront something other than laughter – a film which, even in its comic sequences, never uses humour as an exclusive strategy.

The Butcher's Revolt has its origins in a similar intellectual project. But all of the elements which, in the previous film, had a powerful presence, are now deployed with the very maximum readability: eroticism, cruelty, the taste for blood, research into violence, obsession with the horrible, dissolution of moral values, social hypocrisy, lies, false witness, sadism, perversity, etc, etc.

But you would be wrong to see the sole reason for being of this film in that outpouring of repressed sensations and infamies. I have never perceived a satisfactory explanation for inspiration or the state of the mind solely in sexuality, repression, and the unconscious. I wanted to make that clear.

As for sound cinema: you will see that *The Butcher's Revolt* will be a sound film to the degree that the words spoken are never positioned in the film simply in order to make the images spring to life. The voices are there *in space*, like objects. And it's in their visual dimension that you must, so to speak, *accept* those voices.

You will discover in the film an organization of voices and sounds that must be taken exactly as such – and not as the *physical consequence* of a movement or of an act (that's to say, without any rapport with the facts). Sounds, voices, images, interruptions of images: all of that forms part of the same objective world where it is movement – above all – that counts.

And it's the eye which, finally, will collect and underline the residue of all the movements.

Artaud wrote this short essay in the first half of 1930, at the time when he was attempting to finance and direct a film from his scenario of the same name; the essay was published in June 1930 in *La Nouvelle Revue Française*. –Stephen Barber

Appendix Two

"Sorcery And Cinema" (Antonin Artaud, 1927)

You hear it repeated everywhere that the cinema is in its infancy and that we are present only at its first babblings. I have to say that I don't understand this kind of perception. The cinema is arriving at an already advanced stage of the development of human thought and it benefits from this development. Certainly, the cinema is a means of expression that isn't yet materially fully formed. You can imagine, for example, a number of innovations capable of giving the film camera a stability and movement which it currently doesn't have. We will one day probably have multi-dimensional cinema, even colour cinema. But these are secondary elements and won't add much to what is the core of cinema itself, and which makes cinema a language in its own right, on a par with music, painting or poetry. I've always recognized in cinema an essential quality of secret movement and of material images. Cinema possesses a distinctive element of surprise and mystery which you never find in the other arts. It's certain that every image – however dry, however banal – arrives on the screen transformed. The smallest detail, the most insignificant object carries a meaning and a charge of life which belong exclusively to them – and which extend beyond the value and meaning of the images themselves, and beyond the thought that they translate or the symbol that they carry. Because cinema isolates objects, it gives them a life which is separated and which becomes more and more independent as it detaches itself from the banal sense of objects. Some leaves, a bottle, a hand: they are all animated with a sort of animal life, which demands to be put to use. The film camera creates deformations, makes extraordinary use of the things which you give it to record. The image disappears and at that moment, a detail appears which you had never imagined, igniting with intense force, and heading off in search of the impression you were yourself searching for. There is in cinema a kind of physical intoxication which communicates the movement of images directly to the brain. The mind is set into upheaval, beyond all representation. This hidden power of images tracks down potential forces in the depths of the mind that have never before been activated. The cinema essentially reveals an occult life and puts us into direct contact with it. You have to know how to understand that occult life. A play of superimpositions works to reveal secrets that are in turmoil in the depths of the mind. The raw cinema, taken exactly as it is – in the abstract – disgorges an atmosphere of trance which is eminently capable of revelations. To make it only tell stories, or record exterior actions, deprives cinema of the best of its resources and obstructs its most profound aim. This is why cinema seems to me to have been created above all to express the elements of thought, the interior of consciousness – not so much by the play of images than by something harder to seize, which directly restores the matter of images to us, without any intermediation, without any representation. Cinema has appeared at a time when human thought itself is at a watershed moment – at the precise moment when language has become exhausted and has lost the power of its symbols, and when the human mind has grown tired with representational games. Lucidity is not enough – it only serves to situate a world that is exhausted to breaking-point. Whatever can be clearly perceived is immediately accessible, but whatever is immediately accessible simply forms an empty appearance of life. We're starting to realize that this life – which is too well-known and has lost its symbols – is not the whole of life. The contemporary moment is a ripe one for all sorcerers and saints: a time more beautiful than has ever before existed. A substance which was previously unperceived is now taking a physical form and trying to reach the light of day. Cinema brings us close to that physical substance. If cinema wasn't created to transmit dreams and everything that waking life classifies as belonging to the domain of dreams, then cinema wouldn't exist. It would be no different to theatre. But cinema, this direct and immediate language, has no need of heavy, slow logic in order to live and expand. Cinema must become closer and closer to the fantastic –

and we see more and more that the fantastic is, in reality, the real; otherwise, cinema will die – or, more exactly, it will become just another art form, like painting, like poetry. What is certain is that most forms of representation have had their day. Paintings, however good they may be, have for a long time only reproduced the abstract. So it's not just a question of choice – there's isn't a cinema which represents life on one hand, and a cinema which represents the workings of the mind on the other. Life – or what we call life – is going to become inseparable from the mind. A profound mental terrain is starting to break through to the surface. The cinema, better than any other art form, is capable of tracking the movements of this terrain – since moronic order and habitual clarity are the enemies of cinema.

The Seashell and the Clergyman is involved in this research into a subtle kind of order, into a hidden life which I've wanted to render as believable and real as the other kind of life.

To understand this film, all you need to do is to look deeply into yourself. Devote yourself to this examination: an objective, material and attentive examination of the internal, separated SELF – which until now has been the exclusive domain of the 'Illuminated'.

Artaud wrote this essay in the Café Terminus in Paris at the time of the shooting of **The Seashell and the Clergyman**, in August–September 1927. –Stephen Barber

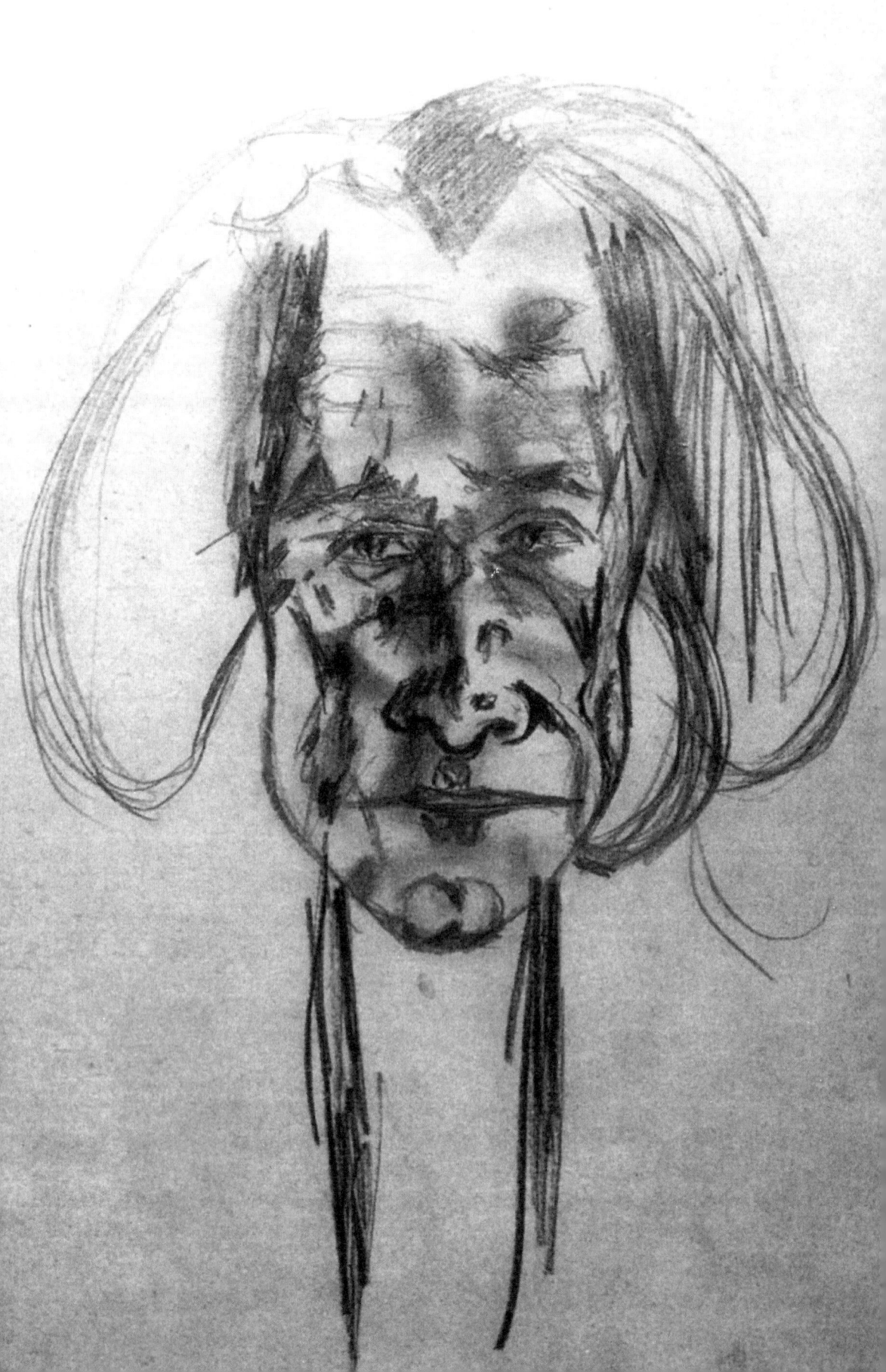

Two

A New Anatomy: Artaud's Drawings 1937–48

Artaud's drawing work is among the most astonishing explorations of an imagery of the human figure. It is work executed with an unprecedented obsessionality, using a degree of reinvention of the body that has parallels with only one or two figures within European art: figures such as Francis Bacon and Edvard Munch, whose ultimate obsession, like Artaud's, was to make an image of the body alive and screaming. Artaud would declare himself at the end of his life to be someone entirely without progenitors, without successors – his work radically sealed within his own body, though always ready to explode out. For the first forty years after his death, his drawings did possess such a unique, insular status, since they were almost unseen and unknown. On the day of Artaud's death, 4 March 1948, his young friend and literary executor, Paule Thévenin, had collected the drawings from the pavilion in the southern suburbs of Paris where Artaud had been living. A small number of drawings were already in private collections, but Artaud had held onto the vast majority of them. Thévenin kept the drawings on the walls of her large three-storey apartment (part of an old factory complex) in the Reuilly district of Paris. Only her guests ever saw the drawings, hung alongside photographs of Artaud and of her other close friends, such as Jean Genet. She would tell her guests that the drawings were fragile – executed with cheap, basic materials on deteriorating, low-grade paper – and could not travel to exhibitions. And she pointed out that her reluctance about publicly showing them matched that of Artaud himself, who, she believed, felt at the end of his life that exhibiting his drawings before a large audience would impair their power and make them vulnerable

to manipulation (he had asserted the same things about van Gogh's work).[1]
It was only in 1986 that Paule Thévenin decided that she would agree to a
full-scale exhibition of the drawings, in the aftermath of the publication in
France and Germany of a catalogue of the drawings which she had compiled.
A full-scale exhibition of almost all of Artaud's drawings opened at the
Centre Georges Pompidou in Paris on 30 June 1987. In the sixteen years
since that time, Artaud's drawings have acquired an extraordinary new life.

It was only during the last three years of Artaud's own life that his
preoccupation with physical transformation led him to what is undoubtedly
the most enduring visual manifestation of his work: his drawings. The years
between Artaud's abandonment of his cinema projects and the subsequent
collapse of his film-acting career, in 1935, and the start of the essential phase
of his drawing work, ten years later, had been a time of expulsion, torture
and incarceration.

Artaud's attempts to incorporate his theories of performance within
a sequence of spectacles in the Parisian theatre of the mid-1930s – the project
which he called the "Theatre of Cruelty" – had been painful failures, and had
left few material traces. (It would only be in the late 1950s that the sequence
of essays which he had written to support his experiments in theatre, *The
Theatre And Its Double*, would begin to achieve their legendary status.) The
"Theatre of Cruelty" was based around ideas of an unrepeatable, ferociously
gestural event, which would combust itself in its act of realization. But, in
the event, the ephemerality of Artaud's theatrical performances was due more
to the ridicule and neglect which they met in the Parisian theatrical milieu,
rather than to their own intention to survive only in the lacerated
consciousness of their spectators.

Artaud left Paris abruptly in January 1936, shortly after making his final two
appearances as a film actor, in Abel Gance's **Lucrecia Borgia** and Maurice
Tourneur's **Koenigsmark**. Like almost all of his film roles, Artaud had
experienced these last appearances as humiliations (in the inane
Koenigsmark, a lumbering costume drama, he had a small part as an
eccentric chemist). That previous year had also seen the disastrous run of his
final "Theatre of Cruelty" spectacle, *The Cenci*. Artaud travelled first to the

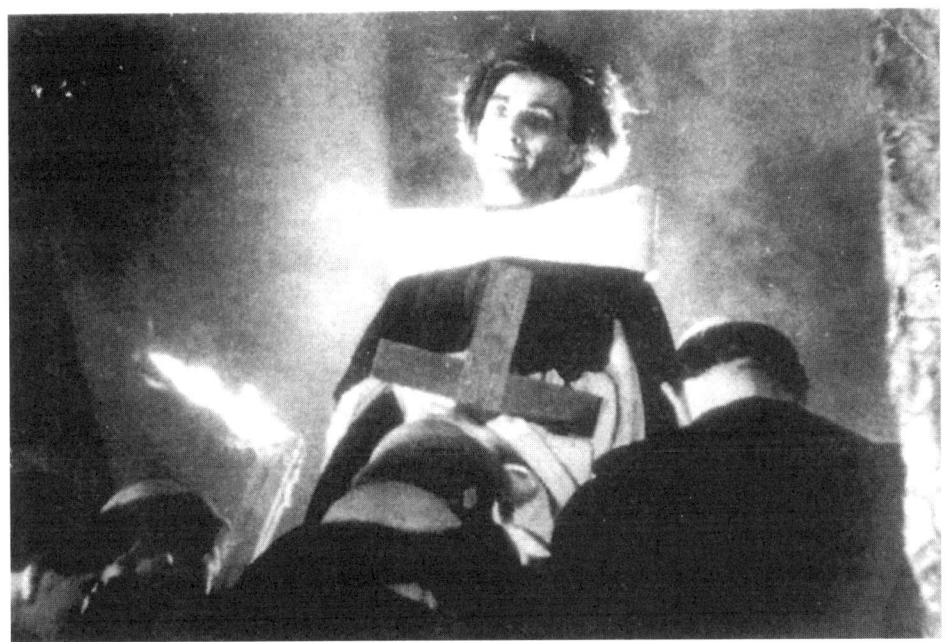

Artaud in *Lucrecia Borgia*

mountains of northern Mexico, where he participated in the peyote drug rituals of the Tarahumara Indians, hoping to find a revolutionary culture of fire and dance which would supplant his terminally jaded experience of European culture. After a brief period back in France, during which he became enthralled by apocalyptic ideas of an imminent global catastrophe, Artaud set out again for the remote Aran islands of western Ireland, from where he intended to watch the end of what he saw as a corrupt and compromised world. He had written a text giving precise dates for the different stages of the cataclysm, and had published it in Paris in the form of an anonymous booklet entitled *The New Revelations Of Being*. In Ireland, he spent weeks in a state of destitution, and wrote innumerable letters to friends and associates in Paris, covering the paper in vividly coloured signs and fetish symbols, and burning holes into the ripped and stained surface with cigarette ends. The content of the letters dealt with his apocalyptic prophecies, and with his own part in the aftermath of the devastation; he expected to survive and to assume a position of great power over a re-emerging new world. But, as the days went on and no signs of an impending cataclysm appeared, the

43

letters took on a tone of furious frustration. Now, when Artaud burned holes in his letters, the textual content made it clear that he believed that he was literally inflicting wounds on the bodies of people in Paris whom he felt had abandoned or betrayed him; by contrast, several friends received letters whose textual content indicated that the burns and visual damage were there to protect them physically from danger, or to warn them of the imminence of danger. Sometimes, a gestural line of sudden cancellation would be driven across the textual element of the letters. These "spells", as Artaud called his letters from Ireland, were designed to embody his sense of anger and isolation, and to exact retribution on their recipients, whom he accused of having failed him.

Once it became clear that the apocalypse he was eagerly expecting was not, after all, going to happen immediately, Artaud crossed Ireland to Dublin, and was arrested there for "vagabondage", in a public park, on 23 September 1937. After being imprisoned for several days in Mountjoy Prison, he was then deported to France. On the boat – in a justifiably paranoid and deeply delirious state – he attacked two stewards and was placed in a straitjacket; on his arrival in France, he was institutionalized in an asylum on the outskirts of Rouen. Certainly, Artaud's behaviour in the preceding two months had been exceptionally bizarre and – to some degree – violent, but many of his friends in Paris saw his internment as pure misfortune, since his habitual eccentricities had been eminently permissible in the Parisian milieu he had inhabited before his journeys. What Artaud experienced in the next nine years would be agonizing. He had been one of the most elegant and dandified of the Surrealists, his intensely handsome features hauntingly captured in the films in which he had worked as an actor, particularly in Dreyer's **The Passion Of Joan Of Arc**. Now, he was starved and beaten in communal wards, transferred from asylum to asylum across France, and under threat of deportation to a concentration camp after the German invasion of France in 1940. His teeth fell out and he became emaciated. Impossible to diagnose with precision, even by Jacques Lacan whose asylum – Sainte-Anne – he passed through in 1938 to 1939, Artaud was in a state of institutional limbo: in one asylum, Ville-Évrard, an immense complex on the eastern fringes of Paris, he spent time successively in wards intended for "maniacs", "cripples", "epileptics", and "undesirables". Most of the psychiatrists who saw him simply dismissed his case as being one of incurable insanity.

It was at the asylum of Ville-Évrard, in 1939, that Artaud constructed a new sequence of his "spells". Although the doctors at Ville-Évrard knew nothing of Artaud's history as a writer, they were intrigued by his spells, and initially encouraged him by giving him a wide range of different coloured inks to use. (After the German invasion, the already dire asylum conditions worsened; the doctors had more pressing preoccupations, and Artaud simply disappeared for a period of three years into the huge asylum's ocean of insanity.) As with the spells which Artaud had sent from Ireland, the intent of these new objects oscillated between assault and protection. At the start of the war, in September 1939, Artaud decided that his apocalyptic preoccupations of two years earlier were now being realized, and he addressed one of his spells – with a mocking and caustic textual content – to Adolf Hitler. Other spells pleaded for heroin to be brought to him, or warned his friends (such as the painter Sonia Mossé, who would die in a concentration camp) of the imminent danger of death. As with the spells sent from Ireland, the cigarette burn is the primary, negative medium with which the Ville-Évrard spells are made: burns, and the gestural tracks in yellow and brown of the cigarette's burning ash, circle and partly obliterate the textual and figurative elements of the spells. In several spells, such as that intended to be sent to Grillot de Givry (an occultist who had actually died a decade earlier), it is the gap inflicted by the cigarette burn in the dead centre of the paper which forms the object's visual core. The spells are intricately designed and lacerated instruments of destruction or protection, possessing their own, strange and deadly, beauty.

The history of twentieth century visual culture is one encompassing a multiplicity of experiments with the status of the surface of the art object, from Yves Klein's paintings executed with a flame-thrower to Lucio Fontana's sliced canvases. But Artaud's spells, in their survival and their exhibition, have a uniquely contradictory existence. Artaud certainly never saw them as art objects. They were intended both to incite an upheaval, and to disappear. Artaud's explicit intention was that the spells would achieve particular ends in the world outside the asylum: causing the deaths or incapacitation of people he saw as his enemies, and protecting the existence of people whom he saw as threatened. They also constitute an insistent individual demand: for the delivery of heroin (the word "heroïne" is one of the few that fortuitously tend not to be burned into illegibility in the spells), and for the end of his incarceration. At the same time, the spells are secret documents, subject to nullification if their contents become assimilated in the social world. They are intended to work like an instantly effective poison that diffuses invisibly in the victim's body, leaving nothing behind. Artaud, in the textual content of the spells, incessantly emphasizes the required immediacy of their action – the spells can only act once, and that action must be simultaneous with their construction, in order to achieve the impact on the body which Artaud desires (injuring the body of the addressee, for example, in the same moment as burning the surface of the spell with a cigarette): otherwise, they fall into the void of representation. The very process of intermediation – handing over the spells to be posted, allowing them to be scrutinized (and their constituent materials to be supplied) by the asylum doctors – necessarily destroys that immediacy. The spells, despite the intricacy with which they were designed and the visual power they possess as extraordinary objects, were not meant to survive. (The asylum doctors often failed to transmit them to their addressees, and, contrary to Artaud's intentions, kept them for themselves, out of professional curiosity, resulting in their eventual re-emergence, almost fifty years later.) Artaud, in his subsequent work, would develop less flawed strategies against the process of representation. The existence of the spells as an integral part of his visual work sets them in acute tension with all of its other elements. They are the presence which both originates that subsequent work – in the form of the series of drawings, often also burned and lacerated, that would follow them and eventually be publicly exhibited with them – and which also envelops all of that visual work in an inescapable aura of violent self-annihilation.

At the beginning of 1943, Artaud was transferred from Ville-Évrard to the asylum of Rodez in remote south-western France, and it was there that he began the series of drawings which would continue until his death. The

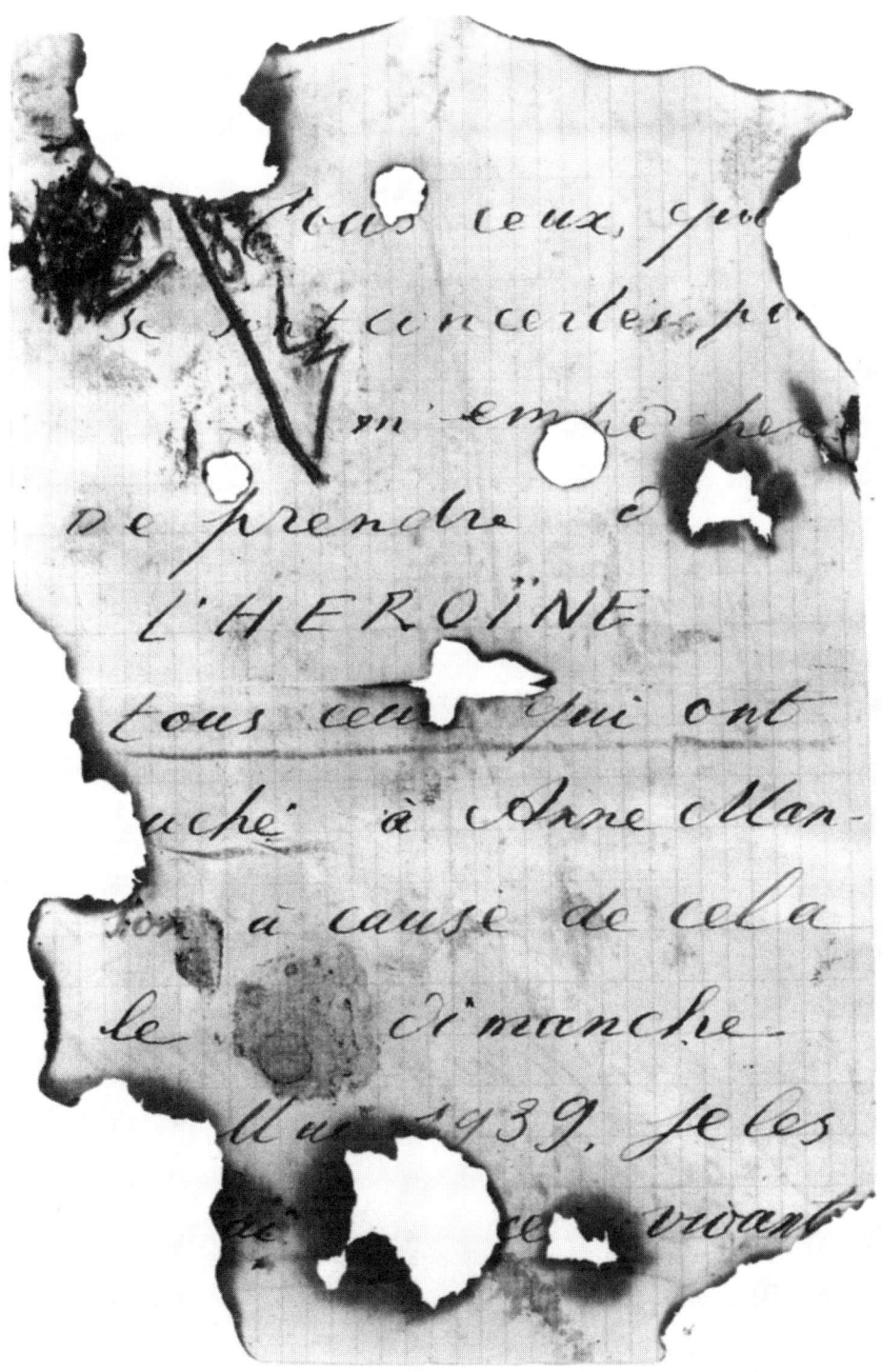

Spell to Roger Blin, 22 May 1939

hilltop town of Rodez was in the backward, rural area of France known as the Aveyron. The large asylum of noisy, communal wards, full of farting and raving shepherds and farmers, had a prominent position in Rodez, located alongside the town's sportsground at the end of an avenue which ran down from its huge cathedral. The asylum buildings were surrounded by a large terrain of gardens. The director of the asylum, Gaston Ferdière, was thirty five years old when Artaud arrived there; he considered Rodez to be a tedious provincial appointment and aspired to return to the metropolitan culture of Paris, where he had spent much of the 1930s. In addition, during the first year of Artaud's stay at Rodez, Ferdière had to spend most of his time engaged in delicate negotiations with the occupying German authorities of Rodez and the French bureaucrats who were complicit with them, making sure he had enough food to feed his inmates, and he also participated in some Resistance work, by hiding people from the German forces. This ambiguous situation sometimes led to threatening situations in which he was in danger of being shot both by the Resistance and by the Germans. He was himself a Surrealist poet who had self-published several volumes of his sexually-oriented work. He was intensely interested in pornography and drug addiction as well as in innovations in psychiatric treatment; a further interest he was beginning to develop at the time was in the art work produced by uneducated and untrained people, especially those detained in asylums.[2] Ferdière had been approached by the Surrealist poet, Robert Desnos, who had been a friend of Artaud's at the time of the Ursulines cinema riot over **The Seashell And The Clergyman**, and who knew that the starving Artaud would at least have more to eat in the rural farming surroundings of Rodez; he would also be in less imminent danger there of deportation to the German concentration camps, since Rodez was in the area of France which had, up until that time, been less directly under the administrative control of the German forces than northern France. (Desnos himself would be deported in the following year for his Resistance activities in Paris, and would die of typhoid at the Theresienstadt concentration camp.) In contrast to Artaud's doctors at the other asylums he had passed through, Ferdière knew exactly who Artaud was. Ferdière's political preoccupations were those of a libertarian anarchist, and his position of authority in a social institution created a lifelong dilemma for him. One of the strategies he adopted to attempt to reconcile this dilemma was always to explore the use of what he considered to be the most radical and contemporary treatments upon his patients. Artaud became the trial subject of two of these treatments: art psycho-therapy and electroshock.

Ferdière and his assistant, Jacques Latrémolière, applied fifty-one sessions of electroshock to Artaud between June 1943 and December 1944. The treatment had been invented only five years earlier, by the Italian doctor Ugo Cerletti, who had observed the pacifying effect of electric shocks applied to the skulls of pigs awaiting butchery in a Rome slaughterhouse, and had adapted the procedure for human application. The treatment was surrounded by an aura of discovery and excitement at the time Ferdière began to use it (although no-one could work out how exactly it managed to produce a beneficial effect), and he embraced it completely, as did many of his contemporaries. The American doctor Max Fink, who documented the origins and history of the treatment in Europe and the United States, commented: "The resolution of the men who introduced convulsive therapy is astonishing."[3] Latrémolière included an account of the treatment Artaud underwent in his unpublished doctoral thesis, *Incidents And Accidents Observed In The Course Of 1,200 Electroshocks*. He writes with unintentional irony of the "theatrical reactions of the subject in the face of his hallucinations", and notes that one of Artaud's vertebrae was shattered by the third of the unanaesthetized sessions. Artaud himself would write of having been literally killed by this same session, and of undergoing an out-of-the-body experience – watching from above the treatment table as the orderlies prepared to take his own corpse to the mortuary, before he suddenly awakened, back in his body, after a dangerously long coma of ninety minutes (the electroshock patient was usually expected to re-awaken from the state of unconsciousness precipitated by the shock after around ten or fifteen minutes). When I asked Ferdière about this incident, he noted that it might very well have taken place according to Artaud's timescale, given the experimental nature of the treatment, but with such a volume of electroshocks being applied in those years – thousands upon thousands at Rodez alone – it was impossible to remember this particular one.[4]

Artaud's response to the treatments fluctuated between abject pleading for their cessation and threats of violence against Ferdière. He complained of acute memory loss, and of the unbearable intrusion of the electric current into his living consciousness. He described the experience of undergoing electroshock to a newspaper journalist just before dying in 1948: "I plunged into death. I know what death is."[5] Ferdière was to defend – and to continue to apply – electroshock treatments until the end of his life in 1990. He believed that Artaud had been withdrawn and unable to write before the treatments, although the volume of Artaud's letters at the time contradicts this. Ferdière was eager to claim the responsibility and glory for all of Artaud's future work. But Artaud's own public denunciations of Ferdière after his eventual release from the asylum would be so virulent and livid that the mention of them alone could reduce the psychiatrist to tears in his old age. Ferdière, building on his reputation as the "rehabilitator" of Artaud to literary society, would subsequently become the psychiatrist of the Surrealist photographer Hans Bellmer and of his companion, the poet Unica Zürn (who committed suicide in 1970 while under his care, jumping from an apartment terrace to her death in front of the entrance to a supermarket). He also treated the leader of the Lettrist art movement, Isidore Isou, during the street riots of May 1968 in Paris. Isou claimed that because he was absent during the riots and unable to direct them (Ferdière made him undergo a sleep cure, so that he was simply unconscious for a number of days), the riots had failed to develop into their expected revolutionary form. Isou and his fellow Lettrist, Maurice Lemaître, subsequently wrote an entire book of outrageous insults against Ferdière, entitled *Antonin Artaud Tortured By The Psychiatrists*. They asserted: "Dr Gaston Ferdière is one of the greatest criminals in the entire history of humanity: a new Eichmann", and demanded his immediate arrest, claiming that he was directly responsible "for all of the social and individual disasters which have taken place in France since May 1968".[6]

In the case of Ferdière's second radical treatment, art psycho-therapy, he found that Artaud was very far from being an ideal subject, since he believed that the therapy functioned well only with patients who had no artistic training. Artaud did not fit this profile: he had drawn intermittently since his childhood years, having taken classes in life drawing at one of the Swiss convalescence homes where he had spent much of his teenage years (his family having sent him there because he was unruly and was suffering from vaguely-defined "nervous problems"). He had drawn theatre sets and costumes, and his working journal for the "Theatre of Cruelty" production of *The Cenci* in 1935 is constellated by gestural tracks of colour from his plotting with a set of crayons of his actors' movements around the performance space. The "spells" which Artaud sent in the form of letters from his journey to Ireland, and again from Ville-Évrard, are a further stage in his compulsion to introduce a dense, interposed image to convey his concerns whenever his written language proved inadequate to the demands he was placing upon it. In Artaud's drawings, images and texts are meshed together with a tense intimacy. The first three of Artaud's drawings at Rodez, undertaken directly at Ferdière's request in around February 1944, after Artaud had been at Rodez for a year, were sparse charcoal depictions of weapons: machine-guns and swords (Artaud had attached great importance to a sword he had been given during a stop-over in Cuba on his way to Mexico in 1936, and which had been lost or confiscated on his journey to Rodez). In two of the drawings, skeletal human faces appear, but they are completely enveloped within a mesh of machinery, human organs and Christian crosses. At this point, Artaud, who had been brought up as a Catholic, was oscillating between adopting his own bizarre variant of Catholicism and a livid rejection of all religious systems; by the following year, he had settled definitively on the latter option. His first drawings at Rodez are a direct manifestation of his most urgent preoccupation of the time: creating implements with which he could violently liberate himself.

In later years, Ferdière would claim to have been one of the great pioneering figures of art psycho-therapy, and of the associated "Art Brut" movement of works by culturally indifferent or marginalized artists; he was involved in organizing one of the first exhibitions of art by asylum patients in February 1946, at the Sainte-Anne asylum in Paris (one of the asylums through which Artaud had passed on his long trajectory of incarceration). "Art Brut" was always a faction-ridden movement. In opposition to the prominent promoter of "Art Brut", the artist Jean Dubuffet, and more contemporary proponents of "Art Brut" such as the Austrian psychiatrist, Leo Navratil, Ferdière's position was that the work of the asylum patient should function primarily as diagnostic evidence for the psychiatrist. Whereas Navratil gave his patients, such as Johann Hauser and Oswald Tschirtner, enclosed studio spaces and organized world-wide exhibitions of their work (which almost invariably had a figurative emphasis on the shattered human body), Ferdière dismissed the idea that the patient's work could exist as an authentic or original art work – for him, it constituted convenient raw material for the psychiatrist to work on, though it might in itself possess very interesting decorative or formal elements.[7] Importantly, Ferdière never attempted to integrate Artaud into the "Art Brut" movement. Artaud was an enormously sophisticated refuser of culture and of cultural movements. His visual work was intensely resistant and irreducible to a movement such as "Art Brut", just as his written work had been indigestible to Breton's Surrealism. Even at the asylum of Rodez, Artaud's visual work was in an incessant state of exploratory transformation and upheaval, mixing media with furious alacrity, impacting image with text, and strewn with a merciless invective against social institutions. In treating Artaud, Ferdière's first therapy outlived his second – he abandoned the idea of instructing Artaud to draw long before he gave up on the electroshocks. Ferdière's personal preference was towards the more benign, decorative elements of "Art Brut" – of which he acquired an immense collection over the years – and he told me that Artaud's drawings were "of no interest whatsoever" to him. The first sequence of three charcoal drawings of weapons simply left him bemused, and he handed them back to his patient with little comment. However, he would confiscate many of the later drawings which Artaud undertook at Rodez, and sold them by auction in 1950, shortly after Artaud's death.[8]

Artaud began drawing on his own initiative in January 1945, the month after his electroshock treatments had ended. By that time, Rodez had been liberated from the German forces. The following month, Artaud began writing again on a sustained, indeed incessant, basis. It was as though he had obstinately wanted to defy Ferdière and his treatments until the psychiatrist had despaired of "curing" or "socializing" him, before then bringing the new phase of his work eruptively into action. Artaud created his Rodez drawings in the open ward of the asylum he inhabited, in conditions of constant noise and interruption from the other inmates. Ferdière had recently offered Artaud the option of a room to himself off the main ward, but Artaud refused, believing himself a more vulnerable target for further electroshocks if he were to be placed in isolation. He drew, always standing up, on large pieces of paper placed on a table, using the remnants of a set of coloured crayons and pencils which had been left behind at the asylum by a Surrealist painter whom Ferdière had temporarily been hiding from the German authorities, Frédéric Delanglade.

At first, Artaud's drawings – to which he gave titles such as *Being And Its Foetuses* and *Never Real And Always True...* – articulated the utter fragmentation of identity which he had endured through his incarceration and the electroshocks. The surface of the drawings became an arena in which Artaud dispersed an imagery of decapitated body parts and organs, screaming mouths and jagged scars. These elements of a physical detritus were set against a threatening proliferation of electrical instruments and machine parts, of nails and spikes. The presence of the body in the drawings was in extreme proximity with what had already wounded and disassembled it, and threatened to do so again in the future. Every point of the drawings' surface was saturated with objects – Artaud associated his electroshocks with the idea of an agonizing void, and his drawings painstakingly occupy all empty, and therefore threatening, space. The sheer expanse and complexity of the drawings' forms suggest the construction of an entire cosmology of terror, simultaneously fully developed and cataclysmically aborted; but the drawings also constitute acutely physical documents. Rather than being the ritual protections and furious attacks which he had constructed with his spells, Artaud's first Rodez drawings simply displayed visually what had been done to him: the elements of the body were shown as a kind of glaring visual evidence, spread out almost at random over the drawing's surface, as though the body had undergone a forensic post mortem conducted by the victim himself. Artaud had been digging into his body to discover what was left alive. In a drawing such as *Box Up The Anatomy*, only the discarded bones are left of the body – but even this autopsied debris can be seen to contain the traces of new human figures within it. Artaud usually inscribed texts around the borders of his drawings, clearly attempting to suture the gaping expanse of his imagery with a carapace of language. However, in several drawings, such as *Being And Its Foetuses*, the visual forms and the inscribed words are intricately intermingled, as though only the random confines of the edge of the paper could bring closure to the limitless confrontation between image and word. It was the textual element, rather than the images themselves, which carried Artaud's protest. The written language was one of furious invocation and resistance, partly made up from a glossolaliac vocabulary of invented syllables. As a protest against torture and as a display of torture, Artaud's Rodez drawings form an exclamation of almost unparalleled intensity. The drawings are all the more powerful for the jarring incoherence and openness of their visual and textual arrangement. They are the work of a man intent on reassembling his identity, but only just beginning to grate together the instruments and materials needed for what would be a long and unfinishable process. Around December 1945, with a drawing entitled *The Totem* – which shows a nailed human figure with a sawn-off leg dripping blood and a grotesquely elongated tongue – Artaud's own name re-emerges as the signatory of the image. But the early Rodez drawings remain an imagery of the irreparable.

It is understandable that Ferdière could apply or devise no structure within which to judge Artaud's drawings. One potential, retrospective parallel for those early drawings at Rodez would be with the drawings undertaken during the same period by concentration camp inmates. But where the surviving works from the concentration camps tend to show the inmates' fellow prisoners and their surroundings – portraits of dying faces, sketches of the barbed-wire, the dogs, the guards – or else represent the homes and families which the inmates had lost, Artaud's drawings are unprecedented dissections of internal agony. They demonstrate no human solidarity: no indication exists of Artaud having any empathy whatsoever with his fellow asylum inmates, whom he mentions in his letters or notebooks only in the form of complaints that they knock over his ink bottles as he writes and keep him awake at night with deafening flatulence.

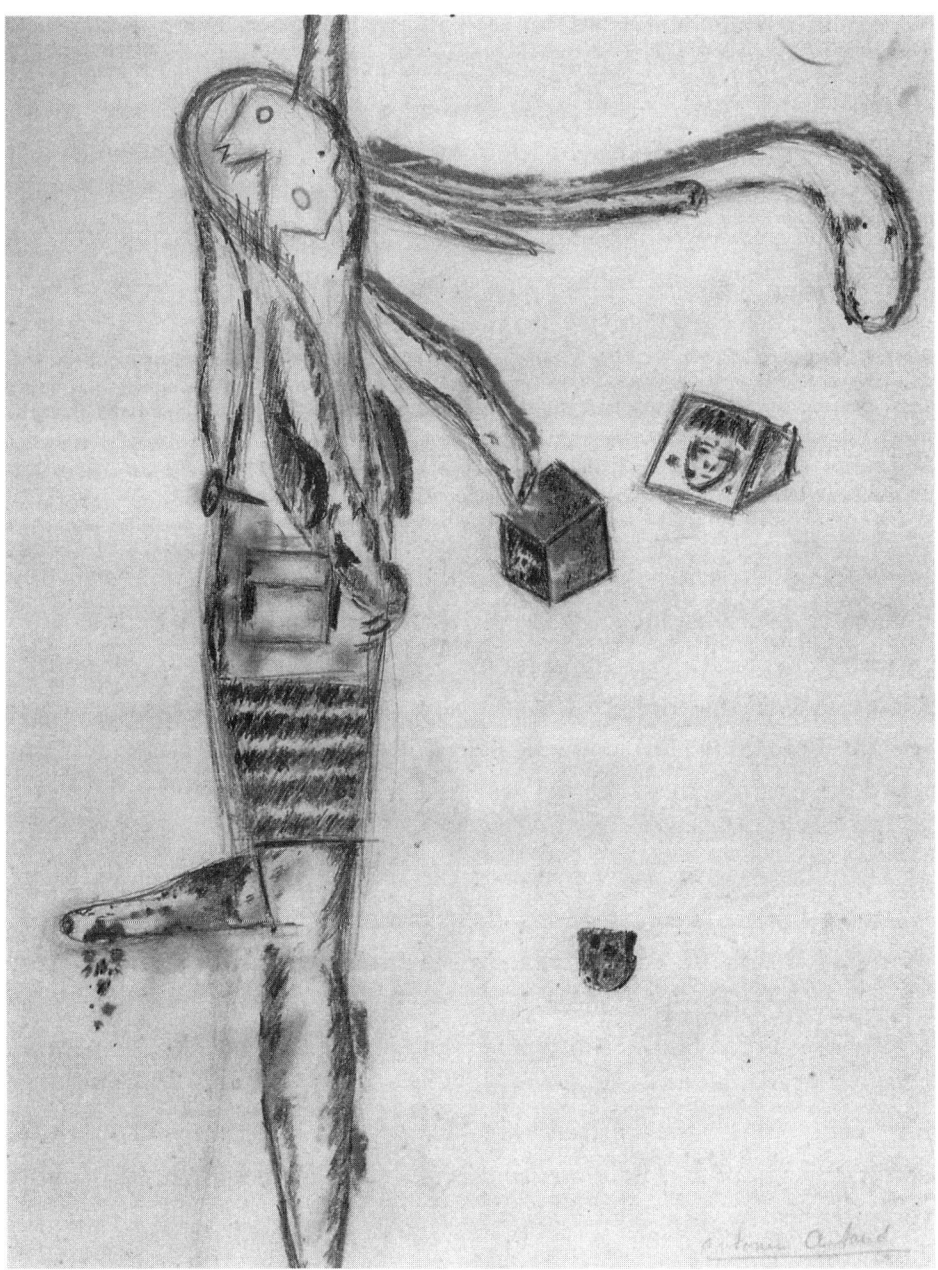

The Totem (December 1945–February 1946)

Artaud's early Rodez drawings project an ultimate experience of solitude.

With the defeat in France of the occupying German army and the subsequent end of the war in 1945, that solitude partly lifted; Artaud's friends from Paris were able more easily to travel by train to Rodez to visit him, and, in the first months of 1946, to discuss with Ferdière the possibility of Artaud's release and return to Paris. The psychiatrist believed that he had done all he could with his dual therapy, and that although Artaud was still, in his view, a potential danger to society, he could now be released into a convalescence home. Allowing Artaud to be visible in Paris would, Ferdière believed, generate attention and prestige for what he considered to be the innovativeness of his treatments. The artist Jean Dubuffet had visited Artaud at Rodez in September 1945, offering him the first encouragement he had received with his drawings, and a visit by the writer Arthur Adamov followed in February 1946. Adamov, in particular, was determined that Artaud should be liberated from his incarceration, and organized an auction of works donated by such eminent figures as Picasso, Braque and Giacometti, to provide Artaud with the sum of money which the Rodez asylum authorities stipulated as a condition for his return to Paris; in order to meet Ferdière's requirement that Artaud should be lodged in a convalescence home, Adamov asked a young doctor's wife he knew, Paule Thévenin, to locate the most suitable establishment.

Artaud's drawings were transformed during his last months at Rodez, when he became aware that his incarceration was close to its end. His shattered fragments of human figures coalesced and became more substantial, powerful presences. The drawings were still constellated with images of exposed bodies and weapons, but those weapons – bullets, drills, screws – were now clearly under Artaud's own control, to be deployed for his own ends rather than suffered. The drawings were now executed with a gestural assurance and fluidity, using a greater range of colours and a more confident use of space (the drawings no longer obsessively filled every last corner of the paper). The drawings also worked to encapsulate Artaud's emergent preoccupations. A drawing from around February 1946, entitled *The Sexual Clumsiness Of God*, demonstrates the derision for religion which would become an increasingly prominent element of Artaud's work, especially in his recorded work of the following year: in the drawing, the

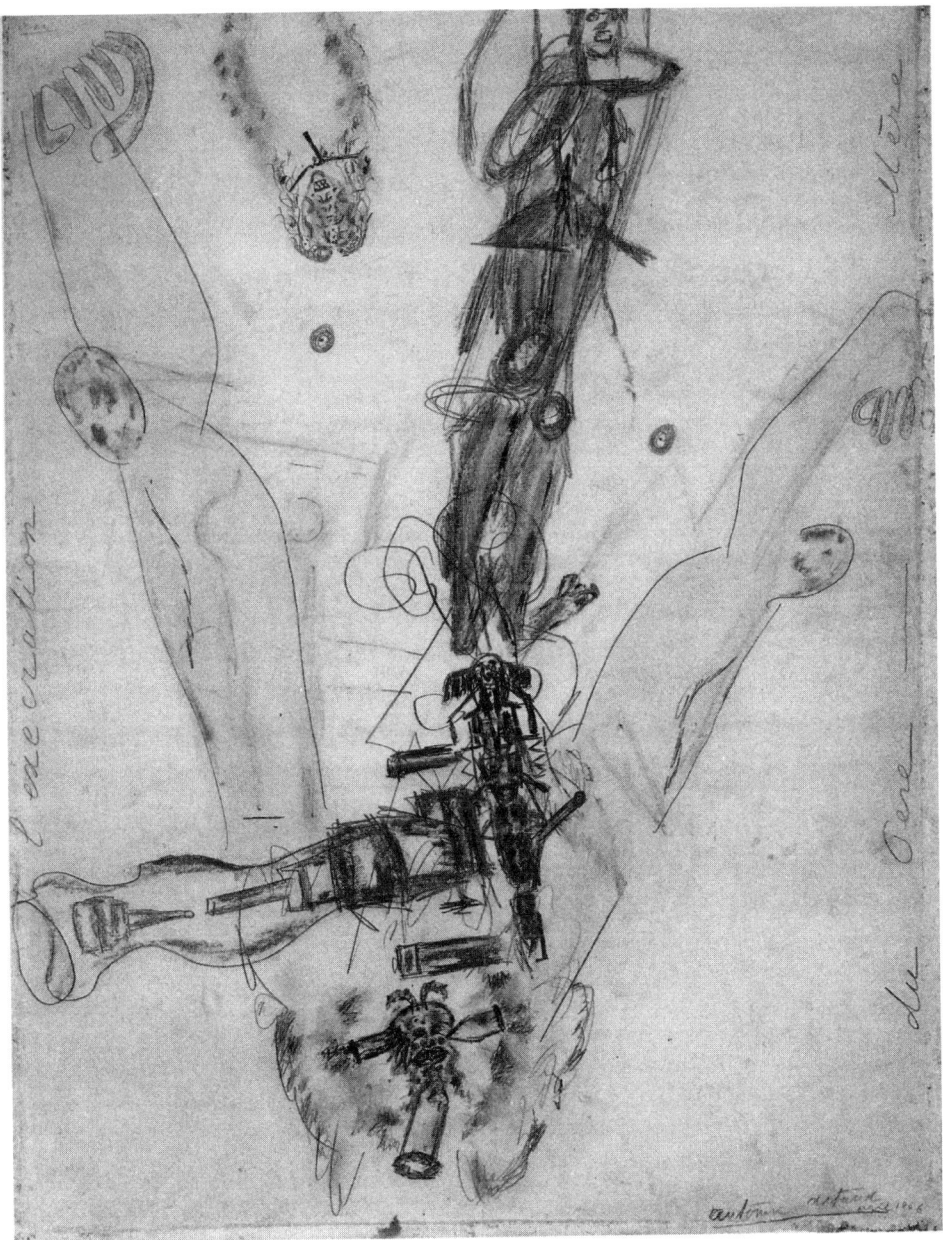

The Execration Of The Father-Mother (April 1946)

ludicrously small-headed deity strides ineptly and blindly through a landscape of decapitated human organs. A drawing from two months later, *The Execration Of The Father-Mother*, embodies the concern with self-creation which would also become vital for Artaud's work after his release from Rodez. The drawing is of an upturned pair of limbs engaged in a monstrous act of birth. The head of the emerging infant is being instantly shot from three sides by enormous bullets; a vertical stream of compacted mechanical implements and body parts terminates in a crude pneumatic drill that penetrates the mother's abscessed thigh. The sex act and the action of giving birth are made elements of the same violent amalgam, which, for Artaud, must be obliterated in order for him to take responsibility for his own life and work, and to fully generate his own identity.

The sense of utter dislocation which had haunted Artaud's early Rodez drawings became overturned in the final asylum drawings by an impassioned force of resuscitation. This was nowhere more evident than in a drawing of March 1946 which took its title from Artaud's theatrical project of over a decade earlier, *The Theatre Of Cruelty*. The drawing showed a group of warrior girls whom Artaud, in the isolation and sterility of his internment, had elaborated as the embodiment of his desired liberation. He named them his "daughters of the heart to be born", but his rapport with them was intensely sexual as well as familial. In his writings of the period, Artaud combined the identities of women he had actually known in his life with entirely invented characters – his two grandmothers, for example, were genealogically inverted, to become feral, erotic children ready to battle for Artaud's release. In the drawing, the daughters are simultaneously dead and alive; they are confined within coffins, their bodies mummified and injured, but they have their eyes vigilantly open and attentive, waiting for their moment to strike. Artaud incorporated into this group of incestuous "daughters" a young actress named Colette Thomas who travelled to Rodez to visit him, and whom he would see again after his return to Paris. Colette Thomas had also been interned in an asylum and subjected to shock therapies there; she later wrote a book, *The Testament Of The Dead Daughter*, which demonstrated that Artaud's friends could be very willing collaborators in his experiments in probing the zone between life and imaginative obsession. In the book, addressing Artaud, she writes: "If you don't want me to be one of your actresses I will be one of your soldiers. If you don't want me to be one of your soldiers I will be one of your daughters. If you don't

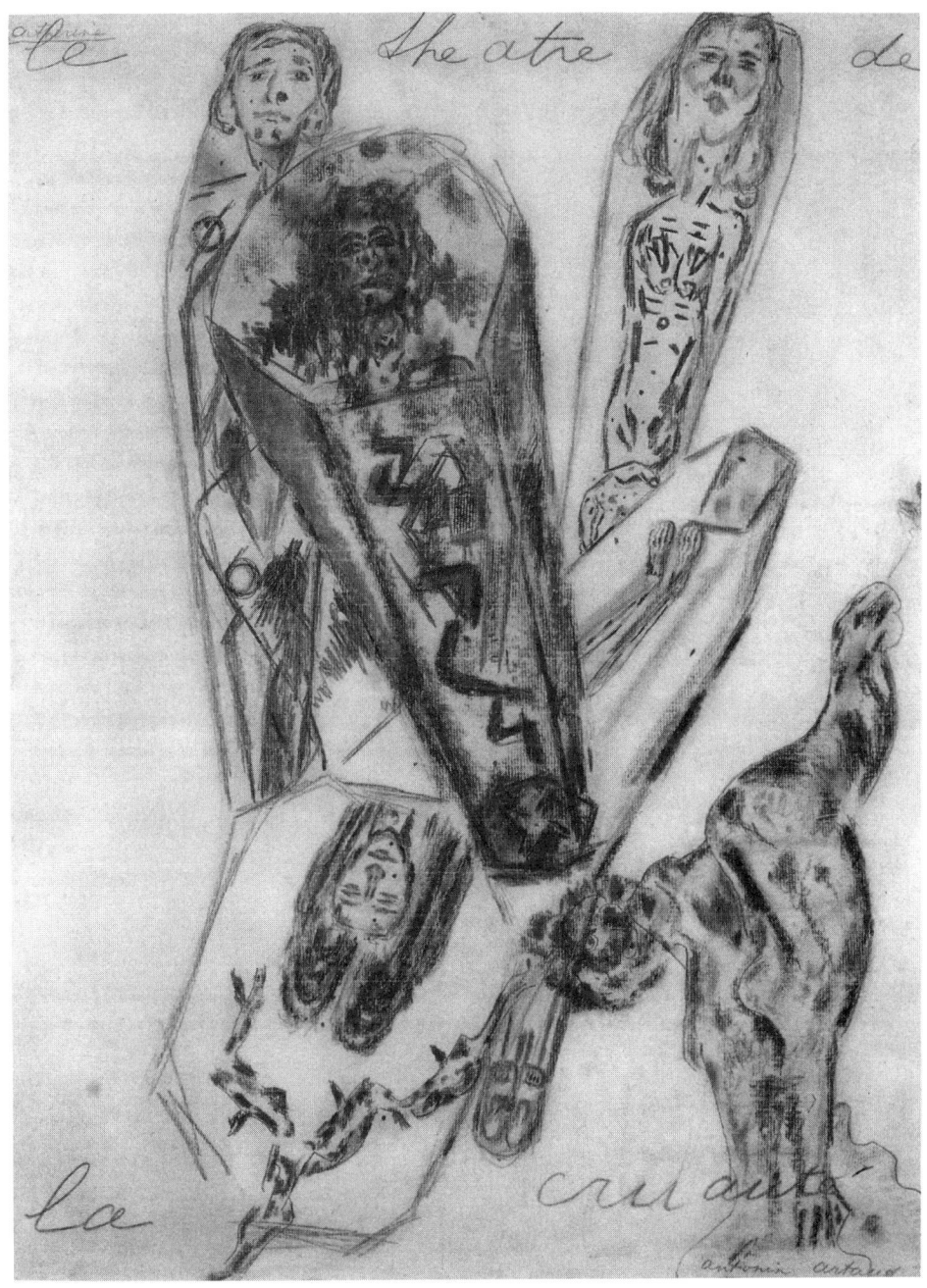

The Theatre Of Cruelty (March 1946)

want me to be one of your daughters I will be your Unique daughter."[9]

Among the final Rodez drawings, there appears a fiercely indented and hallucinatory image – entitled *The Blue Head* – of a woman's face, the mouth distorted and screaming, the eyes witnessing absolute horror, one side of the head eroded away in a densely overlayered mass of pencil strokes and gestures; the names of Artaud's "daughters" are inscribed as an incantation around the extreme edges of the paper's surface. Artaud would describe the head to Paule Thévenin as being one that he had seen in a dream; its visual impact strongly recalls that of the image of the beautiful woman's distorted face in his film scenario of almost twenty years earlier, *The Seashell And The Clergyman*. The very last drawing which Artaud made at Rodez before his release in May 1946 also excavated the human head; it was ostensibly a self-portrait, but it becomes evident from viewing photographs taken in the same month of Artaud and Ferdière sitting together in the asylum grounds that the drawing is a vehement struggle of the identities of Artaud and Ferdière within the image. The face in the drawing distinctively resembles both that of Artaud and of his psychiatrist.[10] One of Ferdière's assistants at the asylum, Jean Dequeker, with whom Artaud was on good terms, watched Artaud in the process of making the drawing, and in his account underlined this sense of a battle of identity which the act of drawing entailed for Artaud. Dequeker wrote: "On a large sheet of white paper, he had drawn the abstract contours of a face, and within this barely sketched material – where he had planted the black marks of future apparitions – and without a reflecting mirror, I saw him create his double, as though in a crucible, at the cost of an unspeakable torture and cruelty. He worked with fury, shattering pencil after pencil, suffering the internal throes of his own exorcism... Through the creative rage with which he exploded the bolts of reality and all the latches of the surreal, I saw him blindly dig out the eyes of his image."[11] For Artaud, the enduringly provocative idea of the "double" was always both that of a force which threatened to supplant and destroy his identity, and also that of a counterforce with which he could combatively reassert and transform his identity. In his final drawing from Rodez, Artaud compacts his identity and that of Ferdière together, in order to dissolve and finally negate the noxious presence of Ferdière and his power over Artaud's life. Through the drawing, Artaud's own identity visually and materially resurges.

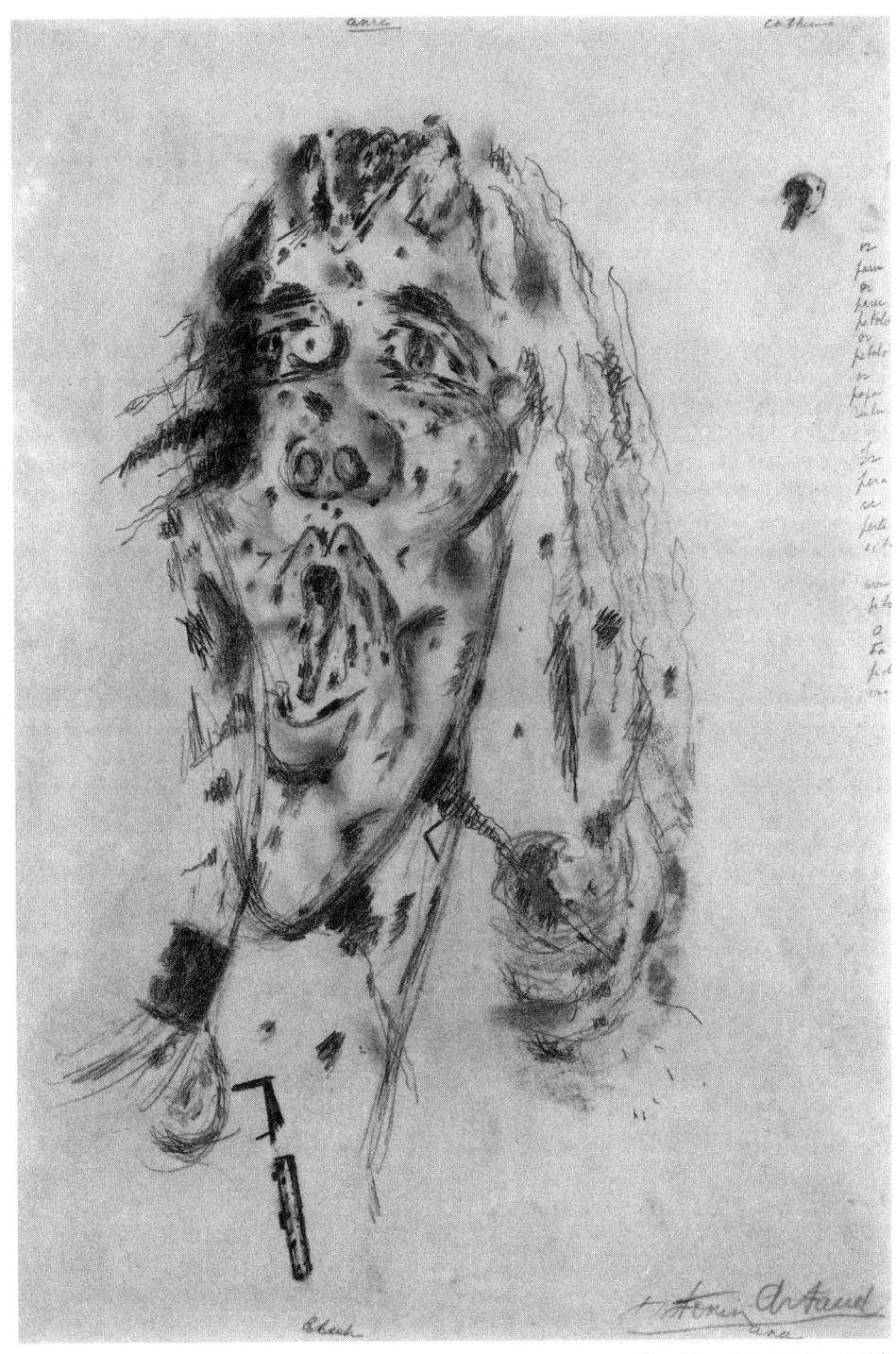

The Blue Head (May 1946)

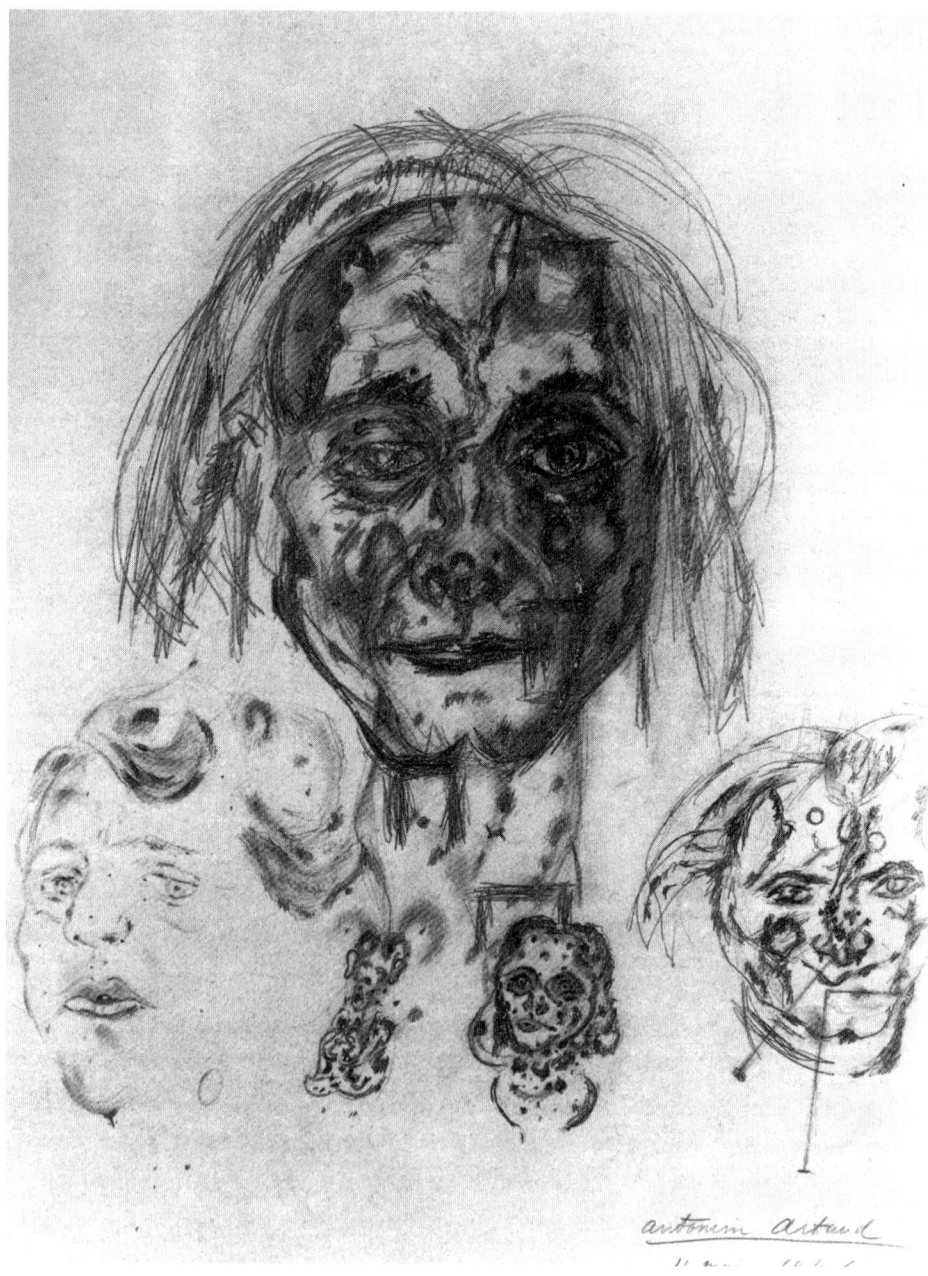

Self-portrait (May 1946)

Artaud left Rodez by the night train on 25 May 1946. Back in Paris, he worked at a frenzied pace. While inhabiting a large, semi-derelict pavilion in the grounds of a suburban convalescence clinic at Ivry-sur-Seine, he undertook a sequence of portraits of his friends and associates which, like the final Rodez drawing, appear to be dual, even multiple portraits. The contours of Artaud's own face, of his bone structure and eyes, are incessantly present in his portraits of other people, as though impelled to break through another identity and to achieve the pre-eminent visibility which had been denied to Artaud in his years of compulsory internment. Viewing a sequence of Artaud's facial portraits exhibited together is like watching the irrepressible transmutation of the same head, accelerating into furrowed old age and confusion at one moment, suddenly becoming rejuvenated and lucid with the next drawing. Other, smaller heads often appear around the edges of the drawings' surface space, like spectators watching the physical transmutation in operation at the visual core of the drawing. But it is always Artaud's own head which is staring, in a face-to-face confrontation, at the spectator gazing in from outside the image.

Artaud was also involved in a constant confrontation with the sitters for his portraits undertaken in Paris. Paule Thévenin became the subject of three portraits, as well as being incorporated into numerous other drawings as one of the spectating heads at their margins. Paule Thévenin described to me the process of being drawn by Artaud as that of "being skinned alive". As at Rodez, Artaud would execute his portraits standing up before a table on which the large sheet of drawing paper (almost always of the same size) was placed; he would scream, hum, and invent new vocabularies at the same moments that he incised his pencils and crayons into the paper. The sitter was forbidden to move about, but was permitted and encouraged to talk as much as he or she wished – to Thévenin, it seemed that Artaud was intent on drawing the gestural movements of her face, in particular those of her mouth as it disintegrated into a blur and then re-cohered in the process of forming and articulating words. The act of drawing, for Artaud, was that of a revelatory excavation into what he saw as the lost or neglected material of the human anatomy. Thévenin was in her early twenties at the time, and she would remember the experience of witnessing Artaud create his portraits of her as being literally terrifying: Artaud relentlessly ground marks and lines into his drawing of her face, until, in a work such as *Paule With Blocks Of*

Metal, she would suddenly encounter exactly the face she would come to possess as an old woman, almost fifty years later. Simultaneously, she felt that her face in the portrait had been imbued with an existence in another arena of space and time – it was a face of liberation that threw out all the anger, determination and ecstasy she could ever feel, through its eyes and mouth. Artaud said to her: "I have given you the face of an old empress from a barbaric era."[12] Presenting a completed portrait to another sitter, a young woman named Jany de Ruy for whom the experience of being drawn by Artaud had been an extreme ordeal, he told her: "It's a head of weapons."[13] Colette Thomas sat for Artaud two times. On the first occasion, in May 1947, he drew a delicate facial portrait which is almost undamaged, apart from the mark of a cigarette burn at the point where the face meets the throat; the mouth is slightly skewed and the eyes' pupils are enormously diffused, but the portrait overall emanates a tenderness that is rare in Artaud's visual work. On the second occasion, around three months later – when he was evidently in a state of anger with his sitter – the image of the face is darkly bruised, bearing the evidence of gestural marks of erasure or obliteration from the flat of Artaud's hand. Striations cut down from the eye and the mouth. The drawing bears a textual element which is in a losing conflict with the image: the letters inscribed on the sitter's forehead (a "c" and a "k" are discernible) collapse into blurred scars and jagged stitchings of the facial skin. A further, glossolaliac text is situated at the extreme edge of the drawing's surface, away from the face. The image of the face is as disassembled and made as vulnerable as any of Artaud's early Rodez drawings of his own body. In its incision of human matter, the portrait of Colette Thomas is an ultimately savage individual assault.

After working on his portraits for several hours in the presence of his sitters, Artaud would then habitually undertake the final element of his drawing process alone in his pavilion. This came in the form of a wounding of the image of such ferocity that he did not wish his sitters to witness it. With the particular portrait which Paule Thévenin described, her face became surrounded by blocks of metal, the face exuding blasts of nails and metallic shards. The facial skin is used as a surface space for the imprintation of an obsessional graffiti of objects and signs. The area around the edge of

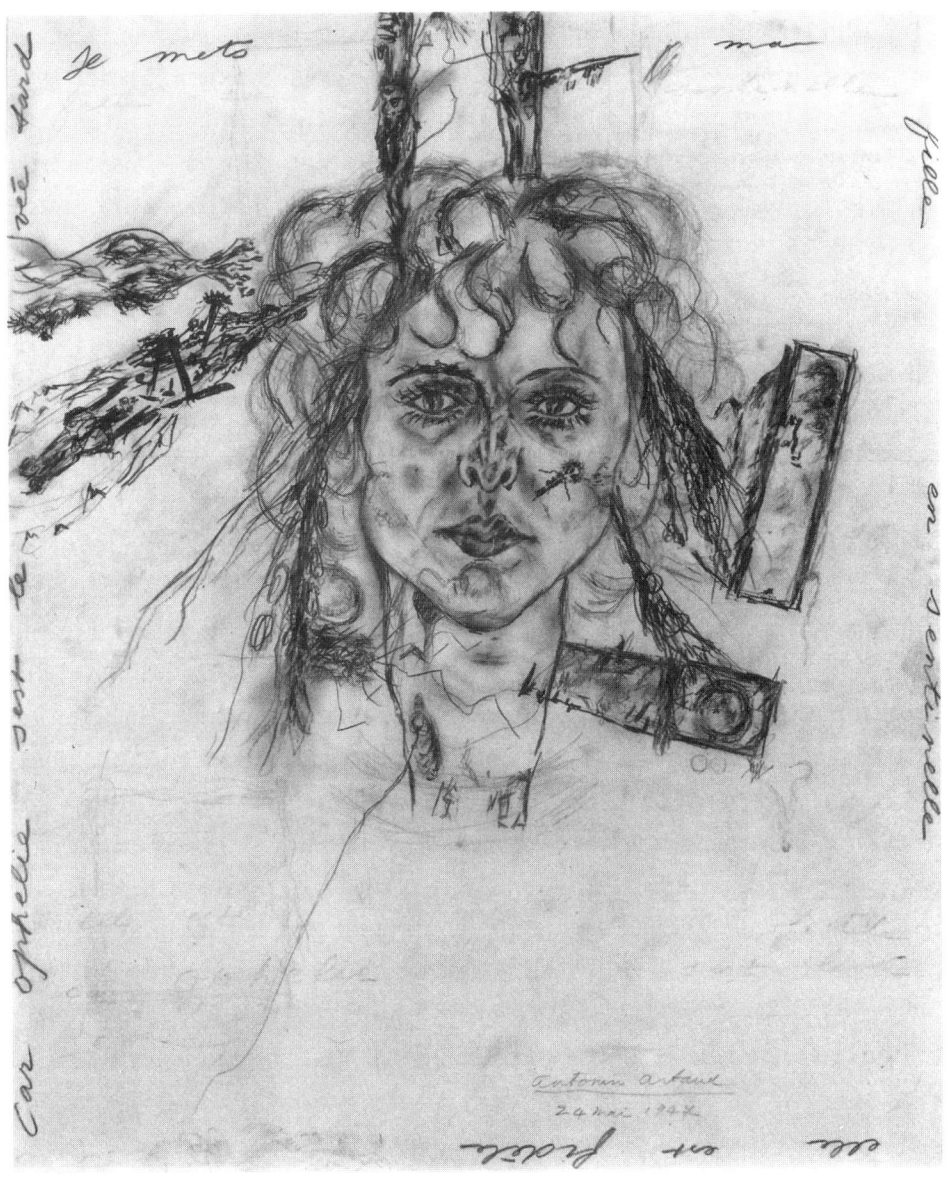

Paule With Blocks Of Metal (24 May 1947)

the facial image becomes used for the addition of a text, which evokes Paule Thévenin's integration into Artaud's group of "daughters of the heart to be born". Artaud's drawings are a creation of physical gesture so intense that they unerringly evoke his ideas and plans of the 1920s and 1930s for ideal films and performances composed of gesture. The drawings of the human face are a further embodiment, on a dense scale, of the interrogation and damaging of representation which Artaud's work in cinema had envisaged; the image is immediately transmitted by the gestures that power it, and by the direct gaze of eye into eye between the image and the spectator. But in order to obliterate representation, Artaud's drawings must always first destroy the bodies and faces of his friends, each time starting the process anew, with a brutal innovation.

Artaud's portraits of his friends accumulated incessantly in the months after his return to Paris. He produced only one drawing that was not a facial portrait – in November 1946, the young theatre director Michel de Ré asked him to make a drawing of the main character in a play by Roger Vitrac which he was directing, *Victor* (a play whose first production Artaud himself had directed, in December 1928, in collaboration with Vitrac); the drawing was intended to be reproduced in the theatre programme, but, in the event, de Ré was unable to find the financial means to have the programme printed. The drawing, *M. Victor*, recalls Artaud's final Rodez drawings with its intricately injured and threatened human figure: the body is suffocatingly bound by a rope of intestinal construction, the legs are assembled from nails and tiny human faces, the one visible arm is severed, and the grotesque head is under vertical attack from an implement resembling a drill or pencil. But the body, lost in its space of assault, is clearly distinct in its identity from Artaud's displays of his own wounding at Rodez. Here, he uses the new visual means at his disposal to cruelly devastate what, by this time, he considered to be the failed experiment of his own distant theatrical past.

Other than this one figurative drawing, Artaud concentrated on his return from Rodez exclusively on his exploration into the matter of the human face. He created an irrepressible swarm of heads, such as the writer Henri Michaux hallucinated about and began to paint himself during the same years. In part, this obsession with the human face emerged from the sheer number of new people Artaud was meeting after his return to Paris: the drawings catalogued them as staring beings with warriors' faces. Occasionally, Artaud would lose track of who exactly he was drawing – one

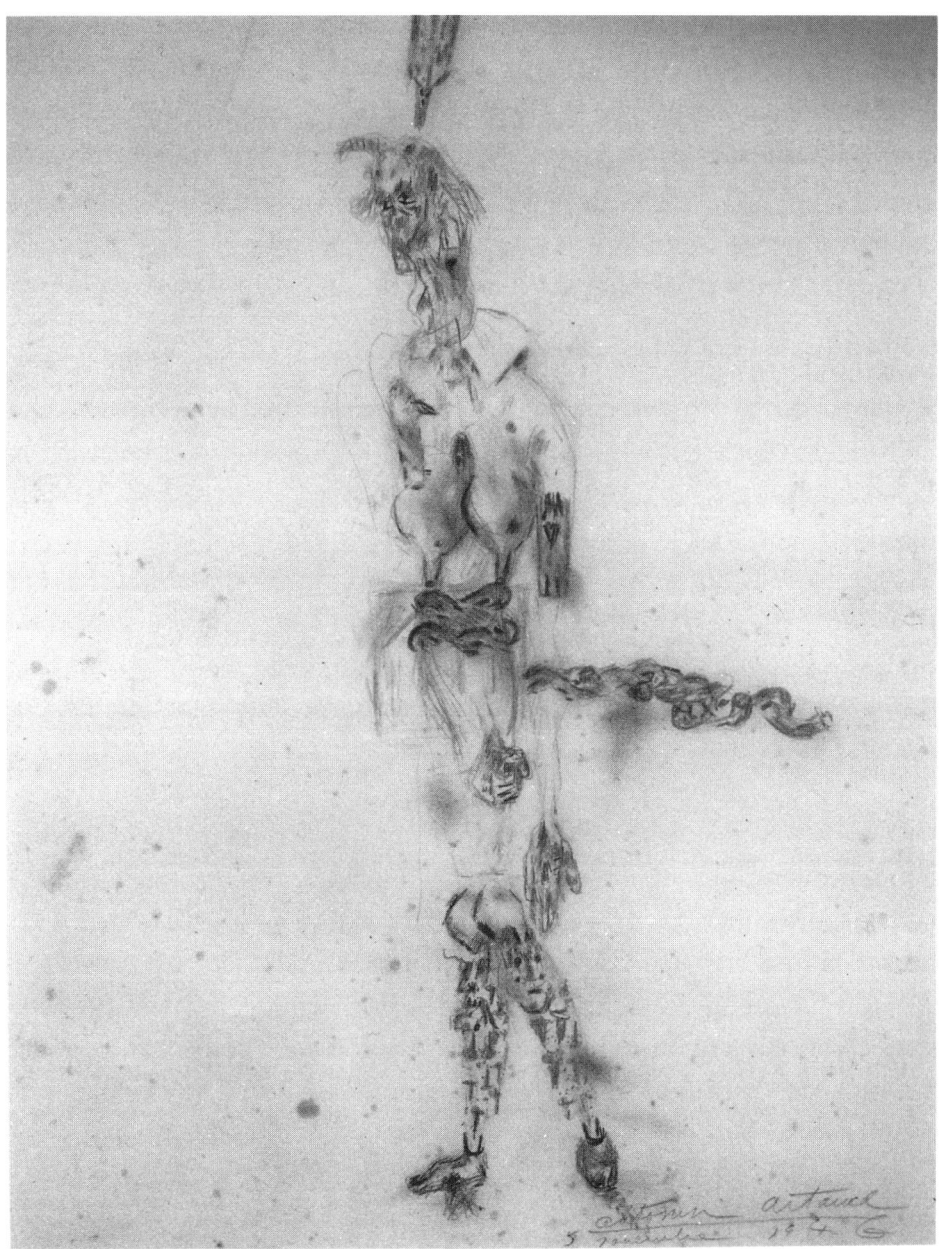

M. Victor (5 November 1946)

drawing, showing a disembodied head in empty space and simply entitled *Portrait Of A Man*, is of a young writer named Robert Michelet who had visited Artaud unannounced at his pavilion. Artaud encountered many young poets and writers during the final period of his life, and a portrait he made of the twenty three year old poet Henri Pichette (a drawing which Artaud alternatively titled a "gris-gris" or fetish object) shows the youthful envelope of the face assailed from underneath itself by an incipient, life-long mass of scars and bruises; Pichette and Artaud had discussed the nature of the human scream during their encounters, and one side of Pichette's throat appears lacerated and spiked, as though involuntarily emanating visual screams of resistance. The textual element of Artaud's drawings, which had been integral to those done at Rodez, remained strong in these portraits – in Artaud's portrait of Arthur Adamov, the sprawling inscription over the drawing, in thick red crayon, threatens to overwhelm the head with its meticulously scarified nose and forehead. The early Paris drawings had mostly been done in graphite pencil alone, but Artaud's vivid use of coloured chalk crayons became predominant in the portraits from the early summer of 1947: in the portrait of Paule Thévenin's sister-in-law, Minouche Pastier, the gestural spurts of orange, blue and red crayon used for the woman's hair spin fiercely out from the head and amass into dense, autonomous blocks on the edge of the drawing's surface.

Artaud viewed this population of aggrieved and astonished portrait heads as having the power of an army, able to protect him from arrest by the police and from the new asylum incarceration which he feared could happen at any time. He decided to exhibit the drawings in Paris, and accepted an invitation from the celebrated collector of Surrealist art, Pierre Loeb, to show them in his gallery, the Galerie Pierre in Saint-Germain-des-Prés. In part, Artaud conceived of his own exhibition as a repudiation and negation of the International Exhibition of Surrealism, curated by Marcel Duchamp and André Breton, which was taking place at the Galerie Maeght in Paris at the same time, the summer of 1947. Artaud wrote to Breton – who had invited Artaud to participate in his exhibition, despite the fact that it was now over twenty years since he had expelled Artaud from the Surrealist movement – denouncing what he argued would be the Surrealist exhibition's "stylized, limited, closed, fixed character as an attempt at art"[14], when set against the sensation of explosivity which he wanted to give to his own exhibition. For Artaud, his drawings were not art, but unique weapons that resisted all social culture while interrogating the material of the human body.

In order to realize his aim of imparting an explosivity to his drawings, Artaud decided to stage two performances in the Galerie Pierre space during the run of the exhibition. Apart from one improvised performance of screams and denunciations against psychiatry which he had undertaken earlier that year, at the Vieux-Colombier theatre in Paris, these events were to be Artaud's only public performances between his release from Rodez and his death. The events involved the reading of specially written texts, the beating of percussion instruments with pokers, and, most essentially, the performance of Artaud's own scream – the scream which he would also perform in the following year for his recorded work, *To Have Done With The Judgement Of God*. Artaud's Galerie Pierre events took place within an intricately determined space: they were held in front of a specially chosen audience, with Artaud surrounded by what he considered to be the protecting force of his portraits.

When the Galerie Pierre exhibition closed on 20 July 1947, Artaud had less than eight months left to live. The drawings of his final months are formed of collections of human heads, amassed on top of each other, laced with filaments of text. The faces in his drawings become progressively more autopsied: they emanate death. Artaud's gestural strokes and furrowings of the image are ground further and further into the drawing's surface, to cancel out that emanation of death and to create a new life through the transformed, skinned and boned faces which he projects in their wildness and resistance. In a self-portrait from December 1947 that is mistakenly inscribed with the date "December 1948" (and so appears retrospectively as a refusal of death, since Artaud would be dead by then), Artaud's head appears composed of the hardest bone, his twisted and erect hand dominating the portrait, with an oppressive head of death fixed at his shoulder. A further self-portrait from the same moment is skeletal in another way: unfinished, it appears constructed from the minimum number of gestural strokes necessary to bring into existence the architecture of a face that cannot then be completed or represented, and must be left openly raw and staring in its refusal of representation. In his last drawings, Artaud drew figures from his past life in Paris, from as far back as the mid-1920s when he was still a member of the Surrealist movement, and juxtaposed them with the heads of the people most important to him in his contemporary world, such as Paule Thévenin and Minouche Pastier. As in Artaud's film projects, diverse temporal layers are abruptly compacted together into an immediate space of the body. Every head that forms part of these populations shows evidence of being attacked and scarred: heads are impaled with huge nails, throats are gouged, mouths are distorted and wrenched with cries. The area surrounding the principal human figures is occupied by a scrawl of gestured strokes – like that with which Alberto Giacometti surrounded his painted figures – through which assemblages of human heads ascend and descend, forming elongated totem poles of bodies and scars. Artaud believed that everyone who had ever befriended him in Paris had been either covertly silenced or murdered (and in fact, many of Artaud's friends were indeed killed in strange circumstances or else died in wartime concentration camps), and these last drawings form a great project of visual resuscitation, in which the faces of Artaud's obliterated friends reappear, infused with furious life.

Although Artaud habitually worked with cheap sets of children's coloured chalk crayons and graphite pencils, two of his final works from 1948 take the form of paintings. On both occasions, this change of medium happened accidentally, since Artaud was visiting Paule Thévenin at her apartment in the suburb of Charenton, close to Ivry-sur-Seine, and, at the invitation of her six year old daughter, Domnine, used the watercolour and oil paints which the child herself had spread out on the kitchen table. Artaud had painted during one previous period, in his late teens and early twenties, in particular executing a series of vivid landscapes – reminiscent of those of Edvard Munch – during the years 1919 to 1920, before he had escaped to Paris from his family home in Marseilles. The surfaces which Artaud employed for his 1948 paintings were also those which, like the paints themselves, were at hand and offered to him. For the first of the paintings, Artaud used a large, blank medical form (discarded by Paule Thévenin's obstetrician husband) that was printed with columns for the names of patients and of the medicines to be prescribed. Artaud's image is that of a body in movement, initially sketched in pencil, and then overlayered with flurries of green and brown watercolour paint – the hair is mountainous, expanding out from behind the body in a proliferating rush. The body itself is transected by a rapidly scrawled text in pencil, which reads in part: "I will eat/a raw child/before all/the world/I the/childish fool". The second painting was also done with Domnine Thévenin's paints; this time, the surface was the cover of a copy of Artaud's recently published book, *Here Lies*, which had been bound in parchment. Artaud painted the front cover of the book, and Domnine Thévenin painted the back. Artaud's dense image, in red, black and blue oils, is that of a body dancing, arms flailing out, the head a mass of coagulated, over-worked red colour; a second head fills the lower right-hand corner of the saturated image. Artaud's two paintings are exceptions in his work in that they are made from a gesturally applied agglomeration of colour that rises from the surface, rather than from the point of a pencil or crayon that aggressively indents its way into the surface. They use paint as their medium to clot together and palpably unleash their images of the human figure.

The most extraordinary of Artaud's last completed visual works is the one entitled *The Projection Of The True Body*, which he had begun at Rodez and carried back to Paris with him. He had worked on the drawing all through the period after his return to Paris; he pinned it up on a wall of his pavilion and intermittently added new figures and textual elements to it. By the time of Artaud's last work on it at the beginning of 1948, the surface of the drawing was dense with amassed inscriptions over inscriptions, bodies over bodies, gestures over gestures. The drawing's space shows Artaud's own figure at one side, and a skeletal figure of bone and fire at the other side. Artaud's own head and eyes, drawn in pencil, stare out of the image, while his body is being shot by a group of soldiers with rifles. His kneecaps are edged in flame and worn to the bone. The skeleton of fire is attached to Artaud's figure by a chain, ending in handcuffs that restrain his wrists. The skeleton is a figure in a state of feral eruption, crayoned in great streaks of blue and orange colour from the black arrangement of bones, and projecting the violent physical transformation that was Artaud's pre-eminent – his original and final – obsession. Artaud predicted in one of his last texts that at his death: "you will see my present body/burst into fragments/and remake

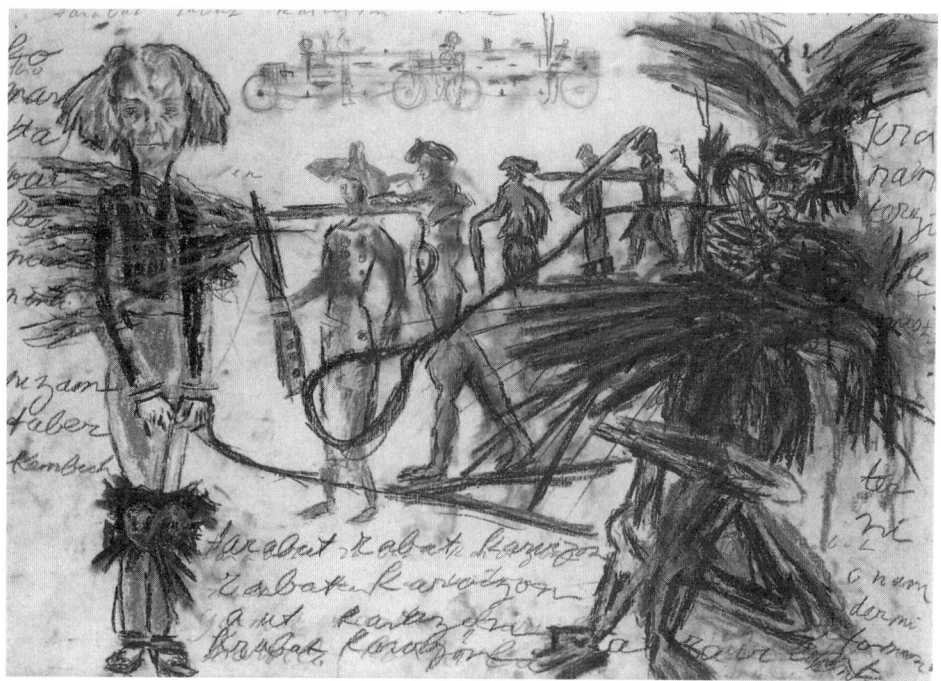

The Projection Of The True Body (1946–1948)

itself/under ten thousand notorious aspects/a new body/where you will/never forget me."[15]

The spectator of Artaud's drawings has a unique visual experience to undergo. Artaud's drawings – in their two sequences, at the asylum of Rodez and in Paris – project a body in utter disintegration and in lucid gestural movement. The first imagery is one of physical collapse and torture; the second imagery is one which gives an absolute pre-eminence to the body as the site of all human transformation, liberation and independence. Artaud's drawings, with their bodies stripped to the bone and taking multiple but shattered trajectories through space, force their spectator into an intricate, magnetic relationship with them, like that Artaud had envisioned for his film work. The response demanded is multi-dimensional in its ocular intensity, rather than linear; it is also visceral and compulsive. To be receptive to Artaud's drawings, it is necessary to come to terms with them combatively, with the entirety of the body, while also exposing to them a sensitivity such as that which emerges at a most vulnerable or unknown point of experience. Temporally, the drawings exist at a borderline moment: one of awakening from unconsciousness with the eyes burnt clean and jarred by the drawings' visual force – a process involving "an unsticking of the retina"[16], as Artaud described it – with a resultant, painful awareness of the fragile or embattled, but integrally resistant, material of the body. In space, Artaud's drawings exist in an arena of seizure.

Over a decade has passed since Artaud's drawings emerged from their seclusion of forty years in Paule Thévenin's apartment, and the beginning of their public existence, which, she believed, Artaud at the end of his life had opposed. Even before the drawings began to be exhibited, reproductions of a number of them (and the occasional exhibition of the few drawings which were not in Paule Thévenin's collection) had been primary inspirations for projects by a number of contemporary artists: Georg Baselitz, with the figurative paintings, including a portrait of Artaud, which he undertook around the time of his *Pandemonium* manifestos of 1961–62; Nancy Spero, with her sequence of works from 1969 to 1972 entitled *Codex Artaud*, investigating the manifestations of a proliferating threat to the body which is so insistently present in Artaud's drawings; Marcus Reichert, with his sequence of paintings of crucifixions beginning in the late 1970s, in which the face of the godforsaken Christ screams in an ultimate abjection and misery; and Julian Schnabel's work, *Starting To Sing: Artaud*, from 1981, which replicates an Artaud self-portrait from December 1947, giving it a vastly iconic scale, but retaining the original image's stark gestural power. All of those projects – and many others – drew from fragments of Artaud's visual work, glimpsed accidentally or partially. It is impossible to know what new experiments the appearance of the entirety of Artaud's drawings in exhibitions will precipitate; but those drawings possess a vital contemporary emanation which provokes, incites and horrifies, as the response to their showing has demonstrated. That contemporary emanation has multiple resonances and implications. Art around AIDS, for example, has dealt with an endangered human body in the state of radical internal upheaval which Artaud projected with his early drawings from Rodez. The final Paris drawings of an insurgent, explosive human figure of anger and transformation embody the tension between a virtual world of simulacra and of invisibly orchestrated social oppression, and an enduring obsession in contemporary art with the body as irrepressibly disruptive or revolutionary in its impact with all structures and institutions.

Artaud wrote a number of texts about his drawings throughout the period when he was working on them, both at Rodez and back in Paris. The texts about the drawings done at Rodez during 1945 and the first months of 1946 are almost always "explanatory" commentaries which had been requested by Ferdière; although Ferdière had no interest in the drawings themselves, he remained insistent that Artaud should write regularly and coherently, and considered the idea of an "artistic commentary" to be a suitable genre for Artaud to adopt. However, Artaud's texts almost always veer resistantly away from the matter of his drawings. When he does directly address them, he emphasizes the intentional clumsiness which he has given to the act of drawing – his images are multiply thrown onto the drawing surface with the explicit will to deny the spectator the possibility of forming a fixed impression or idea about them. He has created his drawings in defiance of their judge, "in order to throw contempt on the idea taken, and to make it fall."[17] But one intention in Artaud's visual work remains constant. He writes that, with his drawings, he has worked "in the sobbing, bleeding music of the soul to reassemble a new human body."[18]

After his return to Paris, Artaud wrote two texts about the new sequence of drawings which he undertook there. The contrary of the Rodez "commentaries", these are texts written of his own accord, concerned with the attempted welding of their own language to his drawings. Visually, the texts – in dense, skeletal lines – form a counterpart to the images of the body which they probe. The first of the two texts, *Ten Years That Language Has Been Gone*, from April 1947, traces the trajectory which Artaud's drawings take through his body before emerging onto the drawing surface. For Artaud, the drawings are infused with his physical substance as it projects them violently out from his chest, with all the force of an expelled scream. And like the scream, the drawing exerts a blow – which impacts multiply, on the drawing's surface, on society and on representation, and also on the spectator's consciousness. It is: "a blow/anti-logical,/anti-philosophical,/anti-intellectual,/anti-dialectical/of language/supported by my black crayon/and that's all."[19] The "ten years" of the text's title refers to the period during which Artaud has felt written language alone to be utterly inadequate to his demands on it; he has turned to the image in order to project his pre-occupations, and also to amalgams of the image with a textual language that is reactivated by its proximity to the propulsive image. But in *Ten Years That Language Has Been Gone*, Artaud is using an entirely written language to evoke the nullity of an entirely written language. He is grating ferociously and stubbornly against his own medium, testing it and looking insistently for the points at which – with his text of sparse bursts of corporeal imagery that aim only to seize the body in form and content – language can be contradictorily metamorphosed into image. In its new manifestation, this language will act, with immediacy, not *like* lightning, but *as* lightning: "I say that the lost language is now a lightning which I make reappear through the human fact of breath: lightning which my pencil blows on paper sanction."[20]

In the catalogue of his exhibition at the Galerie Pierre in July 1947 (a cheaply produced, nine-page publication which contained no reproductions of his drawings), Artaud included a second text about his drawings – in particular, the portraits – entitled *The Human Face*, which he had written during the previous month.[21] This text articulates the set of intentions he worked with in executing his excavations of the human figure. He writes: "The human face carries, in effect, a kind of perpetual death on its face/from which it's for the painter alone to save it/by giving back to it its authentic features."[22] Writing of his own drawings, Artaud notes that: "All of them are attempts: that is to say, blows or thrusts, in all of the directions of hazard, of possibility, of chance, or of destiny... That is why a number of the drawings are amalgams of poems and portraits, of written interjections... So, you will have to accept these drawings in the barbarity and disorder of their technique, 'which is never preoccupied with art', but with the sincerity and the spontaneity of gesture."[23] As with his assertions about his Rodez drawings, Artaud again stresses the necessity for an intentionally clumsy style, which will assault the drawing from every direction – including using the exploratory combination of language with image on the drawing surface – to make it release its essential matter. Art, for Artaud, is stagnantly antithetical to this liberatory gesture; where Artaud had, to Breton, denounced the Surrealist exhibition of 1947 as ineptly limiting itself by allying itself to a pre-existing idea of art, here he attempts to generate a limitless space between his own work and art (even typographically placing the repudiated word within double inverted commas, as though to protect his own language and portraits from it). Even on one of the very first of his Rodez drawings, *Never Real And Always True...*, Artaud had emphasized that it was "not art", but allied rather to the gestural beating of African tribal drums. Artaud's work of drawing is an unfinishable struggle with the body and with representation; his most exact and authentic image of the body is the one caught rawly and suddenly in willed suspension or abandonment, before the malicious process of representation has time to set in. Artaud adamantly scars and batters the drawing with his body's gestural production of it, cancelling and dissecting the face he creates, searching for an image of the body with an infinite physical presence.

In a letter to his publisher, Marc Barbezat, written shortly after the Galerie Pierre exhibition had closed, Artaud revealed the immense scale of the project he was envisioning with his drawings: "I have the idea of putting into operation a new gathering together of the activity of the human world: idea of a new *anatomy./*My drawings are *anatomies* in action."[24]

Although Artaud encountered a great number of the artists who were active and prominent in Paris during the period from 1946 to 1948 while he was creating his final sequence of drawings – among them, Pablo Picasso, Jean Dubuffet, Georges Braque and Alberto Giacometti – his engagement with their work was non-existent. In that final period of his life, Artaud wrote about the work of only two artists: Vincent van Gogh and Balthus.

Artaud had known the Polish-Russian artist "Balthus" (Count Balthazar Klossowski de Rola) since 1934, when the painter had been in his mid-twenties; at the time, Artaud was still acting in films and preparing his "Theatre of Cruelty" spectacle, *The Cenci*, for which Balthus would design the sets. Although Balthus was very young at the time, he already possessed,

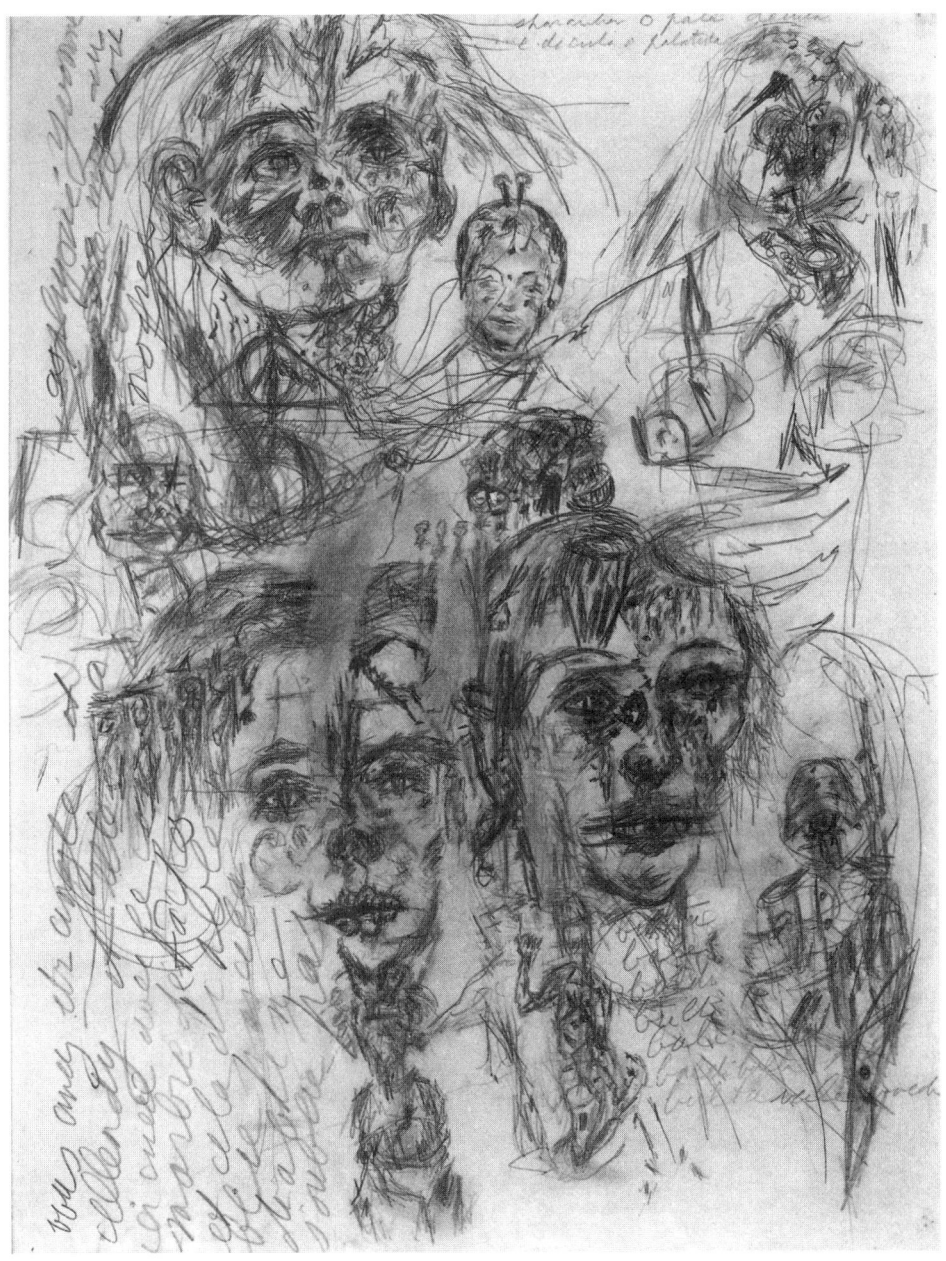

Untitled (January 1948)

for Artaud, an archaic, intentionally obsolete aura: his work had preoccupations which no other artist of the time had, and he was an artist immersed compulsively in his own work, depending for his income – like a Renaissance painter – on a very small group of collectors and patrons, rather than from active participation in the capricious art world. Speaking in 1996, Balthus said: "I am the contrary of a modern man."[25] His air of absolute self-obsession and dignity, with its implicit contempt for all subject matters which would have ingratiated him into the contemporary art world – and its contempt, also, for the contemporary world itself – attracted Artaud to him; they were also united by their detestation of psychoanalysis. They briefly became close friends, and Artaud wrote a text for one of Balthus' exhibitions, held in 1934 at the Galerie Pierre (where Artaud's own drawings would be exhibited, thirteen years later). He had written then that Balthus was the artist "who makes use of the real only in order to crucify it".[26] Balthus, who outlived every one of his contemporaries, would remain a figure who captivated writers and almost always alienated other artists; in the 1980s, the French novelist Hervé Guibert (who, until his death from AIDS in 1991, was often viewed in France as a "successor" to Artaud) tracked down the then-reclusive Balthus to his home in Switzerland and befriended him there.

Balthus had had no contact with Artaud during his years of asylum incarceration, but they met again, early in 1947, after Artaud returned to Paris. Balthus was receiving his habitual attacks from the French art press in the wake of his exhibition at the Galerie Beaux-Arts in Paris in the previous year, and Artaud decided to show his alliance with Balthus in their marginality (albeit two very disparate marginalities) by writing on his work. In February 1947, during the same period in which he was working on his essay about van Gogh, Artaud wrote two short texts on Balthus' work. Neither of the texts would be published at the time: one text, entitled *Balthus*, first appeared in the catalogue of a Balthus retrospective at the Centre Georges Pompidou in Paris in 1983; the other text, *Facts Going Back To 1934: The Misery Painter*, was published in a French art magazine, *Art Press*, in the same year. As in the text which he would write two months later about his own work, *Ten Years That Language Has Been Gone*, Artaud projects Balthus' work as being bound up with an abrupt and gestural respiratory expulsion. But his exploration of Balthus' work is more objectively controlled than his writing on his own work or on that of van Gogh; it has relatively little of the explicit insurgence of Artaud's own presence into the text that dominates his writing on van Gogh. Artaud uses his texts on Balthus to interrogate coolly his concern with the point of intersection between the art work and the human body. To a large extent, Balthus' paintings themselves become an anonymous presence in this process; not one of his paintings (with their pre-eminent imagery of erotic adolescent girls surrounded by cats in gloomy apartments) is specifically referred to in either of the texts from February 1947. Balthus' paintings are submerged completely into Artaud's investigation of the painter's body and of the painted image as a complex conglomeration of anatomical traces and fluids. He writes: "All painters bring their anatomy, their physiology, their saliva, their flesh, their blood, their sperm, their vices, their sexual diseases, their pathology, their prudishness, their health, their character, their personality or their madness into their works."[27]

Balthus' paintings of the 1940s are notable for their figurative coherence and sophisticated technical construction, but this does not deter Artaud from presenting them – with a parallel clarity and cogency – as apocalyptic works of extreme disorder, death and dirt. In his writing on Balthus, Artaud utterly overrules and contradicts the work under his consideration. This sense of contradiction is present too in the language of his texts, which occasionally overrules its own objectivity and veers wildly into glossolaliac outbursts and social condemnations. For Artaud, contradiction is a vital operating principle. This force of willed, irresistible contradiction is present too in the sudden transition from analysis to anecdote, and back again, in *Facts Going Back To 1934: The Misery Painter*, in which Artaud oscillates between recounting an anecdote about witnessing Balthus making a suicide attempt (over a failed heterosexual relationship), and his meticulous situating of the painter's body within the space of his work. In this text, Artaud exacts a temporal manipulation of the kind which gives his film scenarios of the 1920s their disruptive power. He reverses time, and places Balthus' work before that of Ingres and Holbein; Balthus' obsessions (or, rather, those of Artaud permeating those of Balthus) are so urgent that they negate linear time, making Balthus the precursor of all other figurative artists. As a further contradiction, even Artaud's anecdote about

Balthus' attempted suicide is internally shattered: he builds a texture of intricately detailed information, exactly locating Balthus' studio and the precise means by which he had induced the coma in which Artaud (according to his account) had found him; but then, this consistency of information suddenly collapses violently into glossolaliac fragments, with single words split over three lines, and even typographically inverted on the page. As an integral part of producing a discourse on visual art, in his texts on Balthus, Artaud probes the capacity of his language to seize the connections which physical gesture – both the artist's manual gesture, and his own, allied manual gesture of writing – produces between the body and the image. The space and time of the text are exploded and welded according to the immediate needs of that investigation.

It is Artaud's essay on Vincent van Gogh, *Van Gogh The Suicide Of Society*, which is his most celebrated writing on another artist. The essay, written between January and March 1947, was published by K Éditeur as a small paperback book of seventy pages, with black-and-white plates, while Artaud was still alive, in December 1947 (the inexpensive edition, of 3,000 copies, was far in excess of Artaud's other books, which even at the height of his notoriety habitually appeared in editions of between only fifty and five hundred copies). In 1990, Paule Thévenin assembled a special, large-scale edition of the essay, which was published with very exact correspondences evident between Artaud's discussion of particular van Gogh works and colour plates of the works themselves, often enlarged to focus in on the details Artaud had emphasized. *Van Gogh The Suicide Of Society* is Artaud's final work on any other artist or writer: for the twelve months that remained to him after its completion, he concentrated entirely on his drawings, recordings and notebook texts. The gallery owner Pierre Loeb instigated the essay on van Gogh by sending Artaud a newspaper extract from a book by a psychiatrist named Beer, which diagnosed van Gogh along the lines of a vocabulary with which Artaud was more than familiar. Like Ferdière at Rodez, the psychiatrist approached the art works primarily as materials with which to diagnose psychosis. As Loeb had expected, Artaud was incensed.

Artaud himself is the driving character in his narrative about van

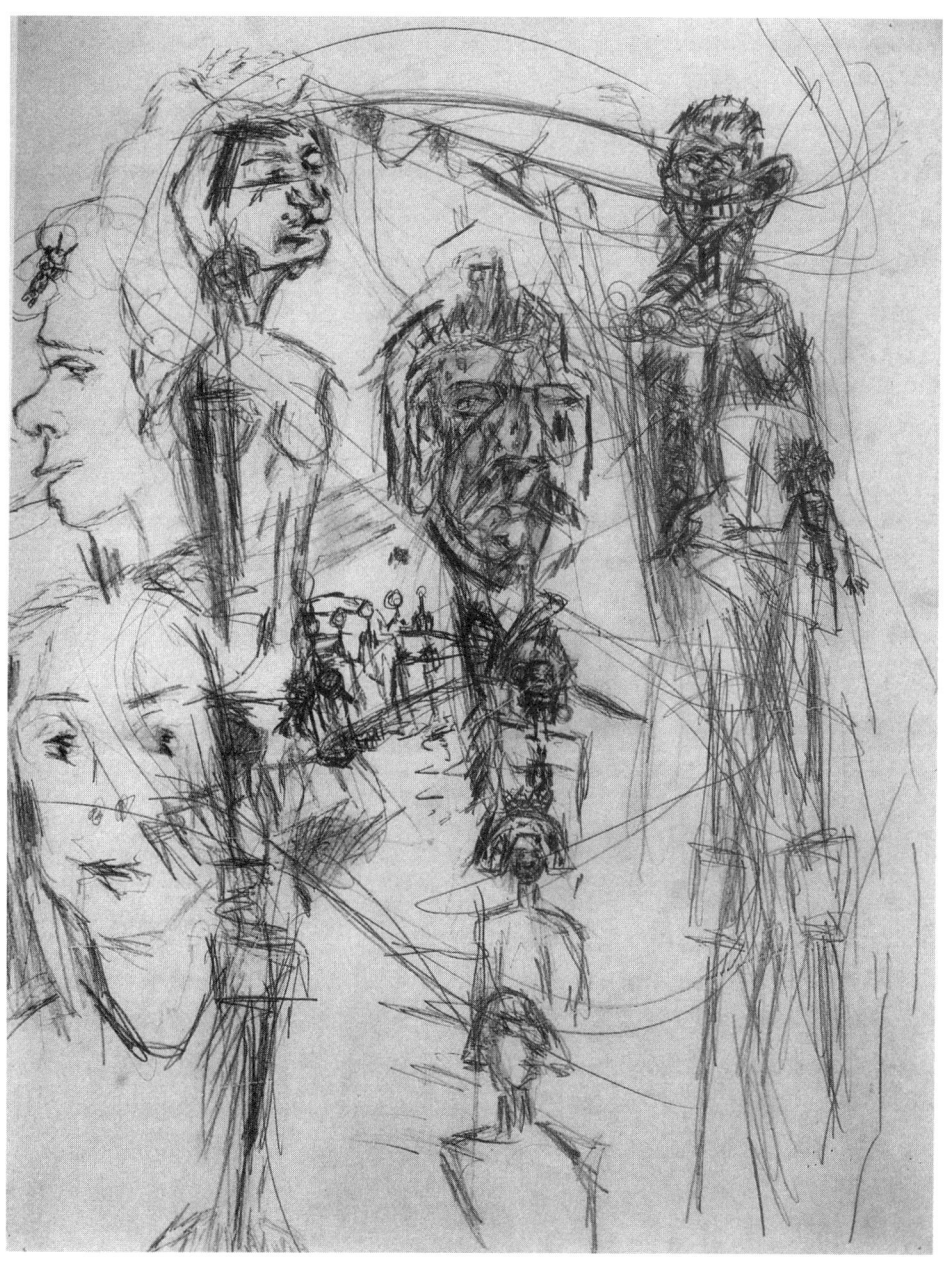

Untitled (February 1948)

Gogh's relationship with malign psychiatric medicine and suffocating familial pressure (these two forces embodying the "society" which Artaud's title reviles). Denouncing both his and van Gogh's psychiatrists as he goes, Artaud accompanies van Gogh intimately on his trajectory towards suicide. Indeed, van Gogh forms part of an oppositional community constructed by Artaud for himself – a community of the only tolerable kind for him, made up from writers (including figures such as Nietzsche, Nerval, Lautréamont and Rimbaud) who never met one another and for whom all social communities were sources of deep antipathy. For Artaud, who highly prized van Gogh's letters to his brother Théo (whom Artaud casts as an enemy), van Gogh is as great a writer as he is a painter – his textual and visual work forming a dense, volatile and interpenetrating amalgam – and so can be placed within his community of writers. The reader of Artaud's essay is simultaneously seduced by the vivid evocations of van Gogh's paintings, and invocatively stigmatized for forming part of the social community which has tormented van Gogh and intentionally precipitated his suicide. At one point, Artaud seems to ally himself with the reader, declaring: "because are we not all, like poor van Gogh himself, suicides of society!"[28] – but this tenuous alliance is soon overturned, and the reader again is the focus of accusations and challenges. Like the spectator of Artaud's cinema and of his drawings, the reader of his language is sensorially and physically magnetized and enmeshed, but savagely assaulted too, in the eye.

Artaud emphasizes above all the gesturality of van Gogh's work: the painter digs at the image to virulently bring forth the body of his subject. Artaud tracks his own linguistic, gestural movement as he himself digs into the process of van Gogh's creative act: "I pierce, I recapture, I scrutinize, I strike, I unseal...".[29] Such listings of abrasive actions are almost identical to those Artaud uses, in *Ten Years That Language Has Been Gone* and *The Human Face*, to evoke his own act of drawing as well as his act of writing, both of which are presented as intensely combative in their grinding of the matter of language and image. In the end, Artaud always brings his exploration of van Gogh inexorably back to himself. He curtails the essay with the image of a huge rock being blasted into a Parisian street from a volcanic eruption. The impact is that of Artaud himself, returning to Paris from Rodez. Van Gogh is obliterated.

The interaction between language and image in Artaud's work is most powerfully at stake in the pages of the schoolchildren's notebooks which he made use of, on a daily basis, between February 1945 and March 1948. Aside from letters sent to friends, the first and last words that Artaud wrote – from the point when he broke the silence of his incarceration, until the moment of his death – were inscribed in the notebooks, in fountain-pen ink and graphite pencil. Throughout that time, drawings executed in the same media accompanied the texts in the notebooks. Over the years, hundreds of the notebooks piled up beside Artaud's bed in his ward at the asylum of Rodez, and then in a trunk at his pavilion in Paris. It was during the two periods when Artaud was most absorbed in producing his drawings – around May 1947, when he was intensively compiling his wounded portrait heads in anticipation of the Galerie Pierre exhibition, and around December 1947, when he was creating his final totems of amassed heads and completing *The Projection Of The True Body* – that the border between image and text in the notebook pages was, concurrently, most strenuously probed and set into upheaval. The texts are often then arranged as glossolalia, in visually dense, almost figurative arrangements of letters: the glossolalia, for Artaud, are expelled from the body, and are situated between language and the image. After Artaud's death, Paule Thévenin would publish the vast majority of the texts from the notebooks as eleven volumes of Artaud's *Collected Works* (the final published volume, from 1994, ended with the notebooks from February 1947, although prior to her death in the previous year she had transcribed and prepared for publication the contents of the notebooks up to the end of May 1947). In these volumes, Thévenin notes the position of the drawings within the arrangement of each notebook page and gives a brief description of the image. But this strategy carries nothing of the ferocious, endless confrontation of language with image that the notebooks project. Artaud himself, shortly before his death, had envisaged the publication of a catalogue that would have reproduced fifty pages from his notebooks. He wrote an introduction at the end of January 1948 for the proposed volume, to be entitled *50 Drawings To Assassinate Magic*, which explored the way in which it was often the drawings, constellated over his notebook pages, that generated his textual language, rather than the other way round; but, once

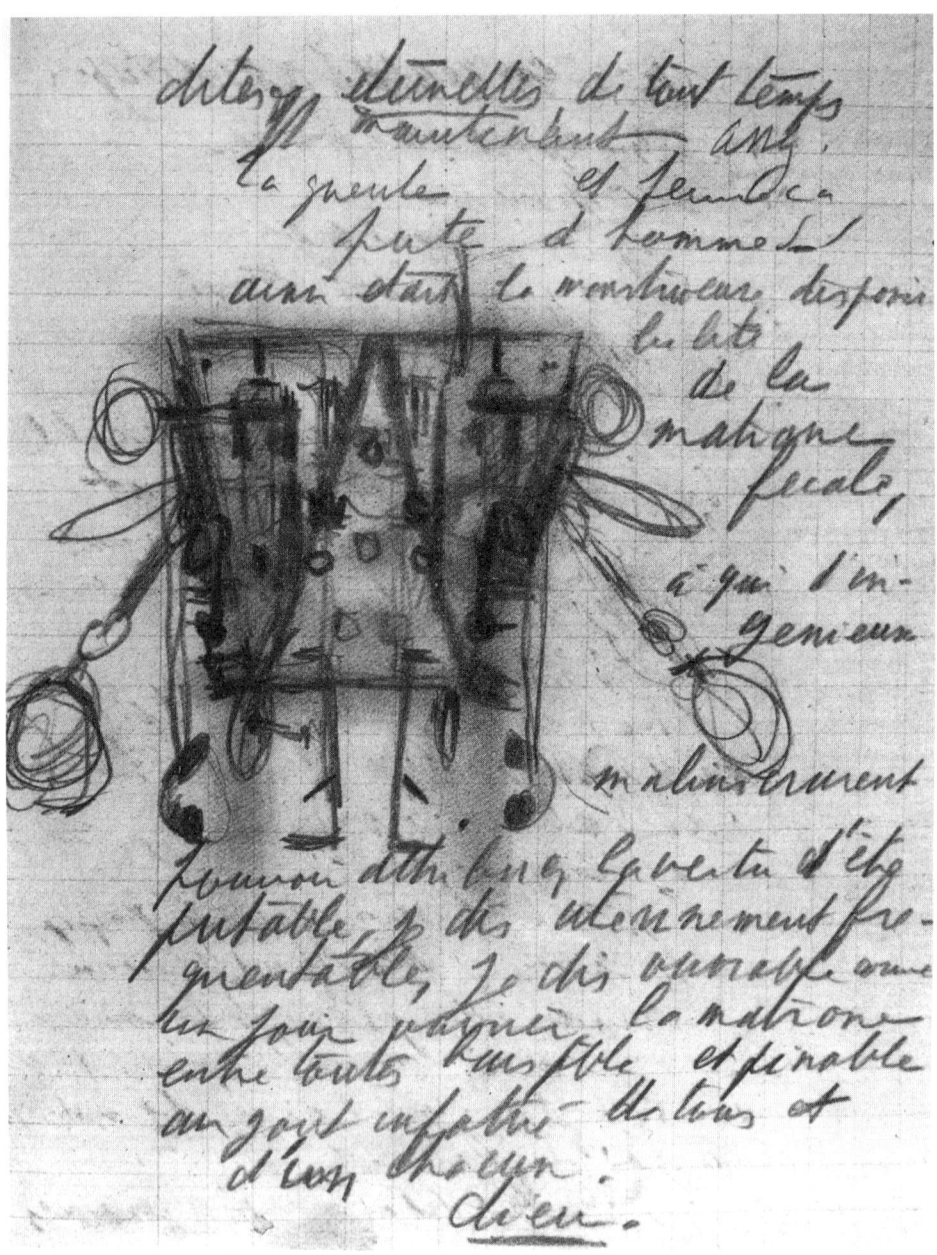

Notebook page, April 1947

his language had taken on its own existence, it would act back violently on the image, precipitating a virulent, vital battle to seize the point of origin for the body's gestures. He wrote that, above all, these confrontational assemblages of image and text were aimed at creating a language of the body: they "will make their apocalypse/because they've said too much to be born/and said too much in being born/not to be reborn/and to take a body/and so authentically."[30] The first of Artaud's two texts on his drawings, *Ten Years That Language Has Been Gone*, also concerns his intention of instilling a raw physical presence in his notebook pages, through his construction of their internally abrasive visual and textual design. In the event, Artaud was not able to assemble the projected catalogue of his notebook pages, since he died a month or so after the project's formulation.[31] Following Paule Thévenin's death, the vast collection of Artaud's notebooks was stored in the French National Library in Paris.

The most striking visual element of Artaud's notebook pages is that they directly convey the tangible substance of writing and drawing as one of warfare. The hand and the material of the paper have evidently been in a sustained battle of attack and resistance. The pages are jaggedly indented and ripped, their gestural struggle forming a counterpoint to the collision between the presences of image and text. Often, this rhythm of indentation, laceration and manual impact will accumulate and fluctuate over the course of a notebook, producing a kind of legible, extended narrative of the body's gestures in their intensification, arrest and reconstitution. The texts and drawings in the notebooks have clearly been executed at high speed – yet another manifestation of Artaud's determination to elude the process of representation – and it is through this velocity of inscription that the pages are torn. Especially in the notebooks from the final months of Artaud's life, the pages emanate a disintegrating body rushing to formulate its last obsession, instantly, with the resulting blur of speed in the figures and words itself forming an integral part of the obsession. Often, the tip of the pencil has broken, and the cracked wood has moved into the surface of the paper, so that a word or image may be visible negatively, discernible only in the cuts and furrows in the page. The metal nib of the pen also carries its multiple trajectories destructively into the paper's surface, particularly when the ink dries up but the momentum of the hand is unstoppable. In addition, the pencil and ink marks are often smudged, overlayered and intercrossed with one another in intricate strata that have been produced by the gestural

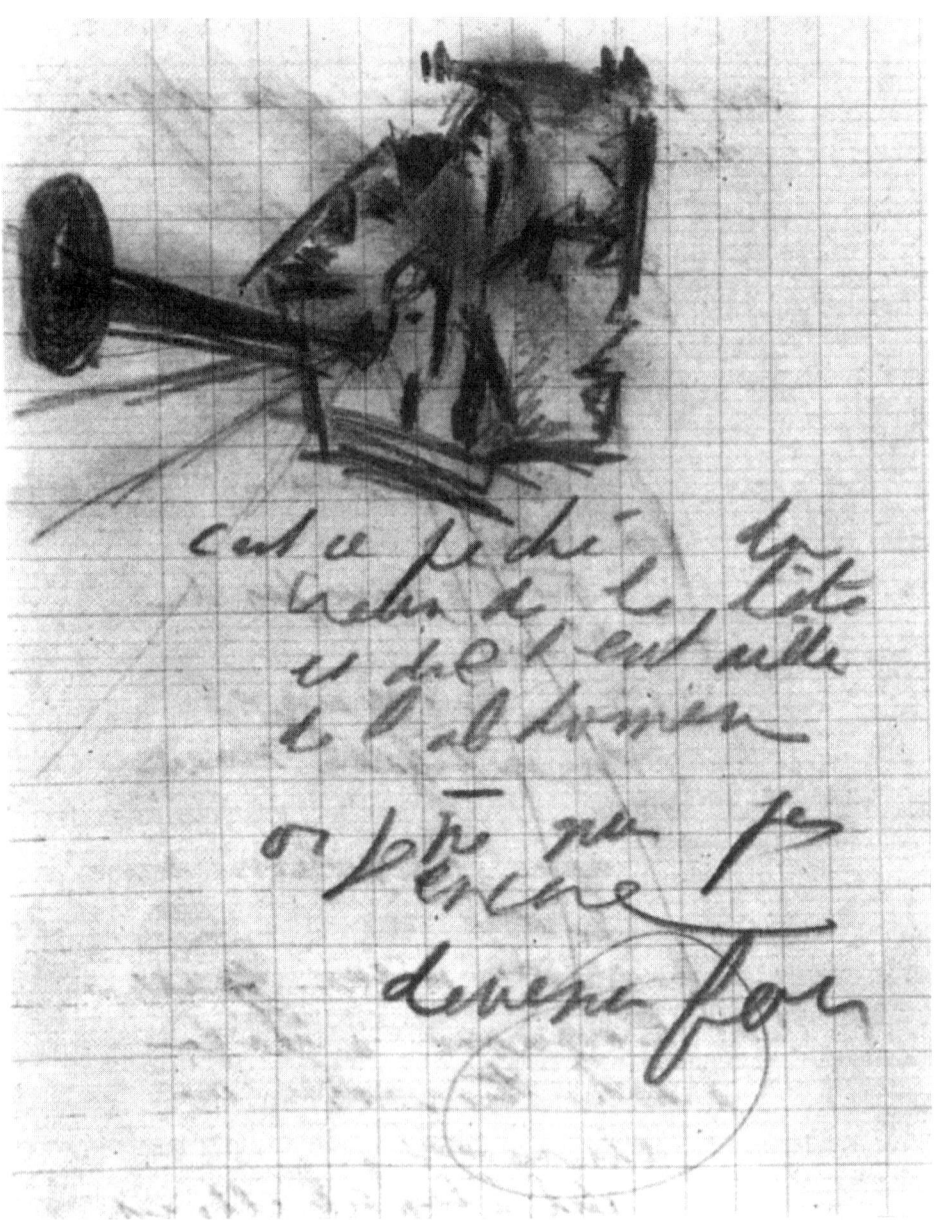

Notebook page, April 1947

movements of the hand directly onto the page.

The space of the notebook page is one of oscillation, of lost and won ground, of supplantation and transformation between image and text. On

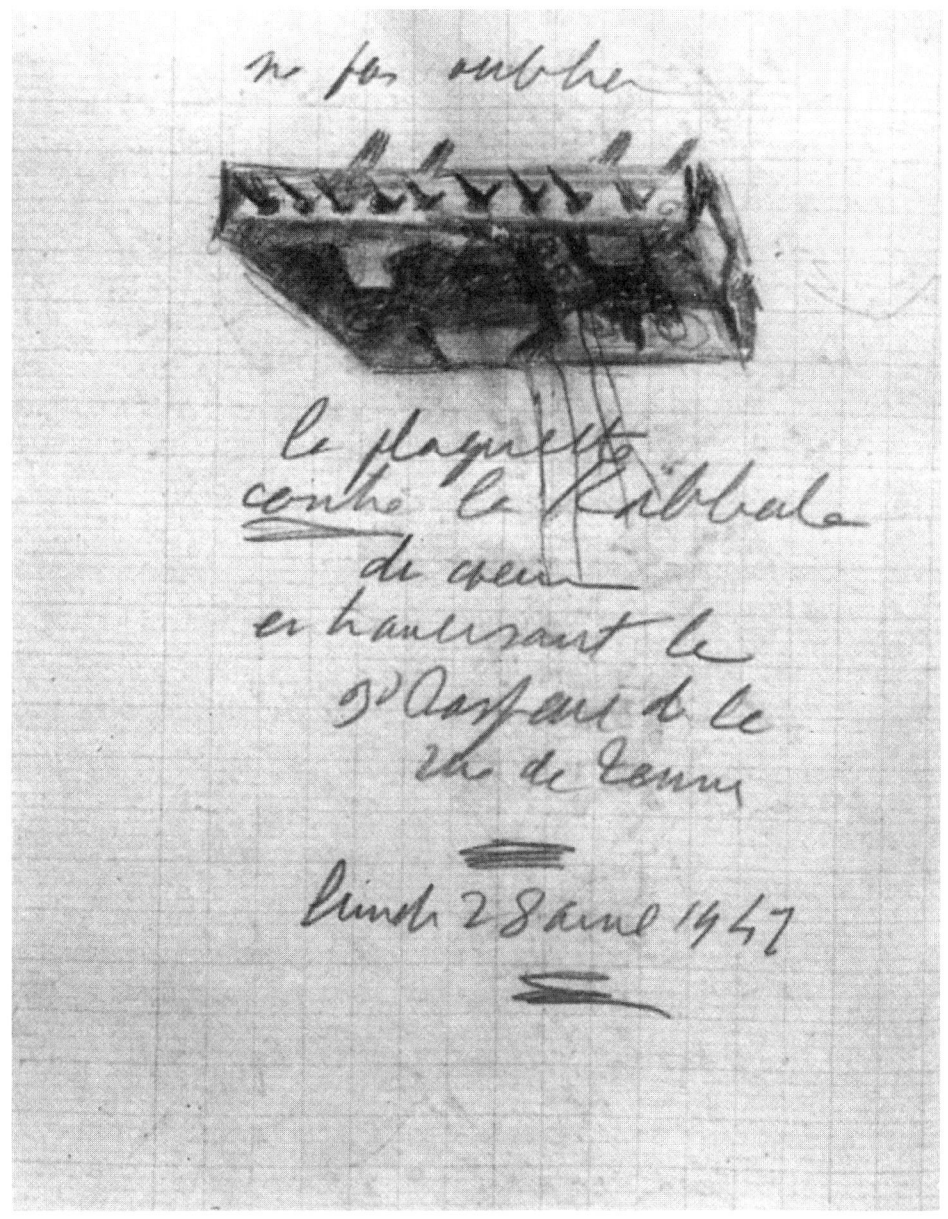

Notebook page, April 1947

one page, the drawings (particularly those of the face and the dancing body) will crowd out their accompanying texts into the extreme edge of the paper's surface; on the next page, the text will proliferate expansively and expel the image away to a peripheral zone. Sometimes, the preoccupations of image and text will be allied – the text will invoke weapons and anger, and the images will be of nails, broken bones and instruments of torture – and at other times, the two contents are divergent, contradictory or in confrontation. In a notebook page from June 1947, the text condensed at the top of the surface space reads: "they are digested/they are assimilated/shit is made of them/they are made to rot/they are shat out again". The remainder of the page's surface space is saturated with images of damaged organs, insects, limbs, and a tiny self-portrait held in a circular, anal shape. Here, the textual protest against the forcible, execrable appropriation by an exterior power of the body's elements is opened out visually, with a swarm of threatening forms that both demonstrate that threat and stigmatize it. A further collision which the notebook pages embody is that between excessively over-loaded space and the sudden apparition of blank space. In its intricate arena for the crash between image and language, Artaud's notebook page has a space that is densely determined, even when void, and a time that is always immediate.

The intersection between the image and the text is the site where Artaud excavates the human body. In his notebooks, it is through the interpenetration of image and text, on the damaged, over-inscribed and effaced surface of the paper, that the human body which is Artaud's obsession becomes gesturally captured. But, at the end of Artaud's visual work, a further, explosive dimension is added to this endless seizure of the body: the scream.

NOTES

The most comprehensive catalogue of Artaud's drawings is *Antonin Artaud: Dessins Et Portraits*, by Paule Thévenin and Jacques Derrida, Éditions Gallimard, Paris, 1986; a German-language edition appeared, also in 1986, with Schirmer/Mosel Verlag, Munich. Catalogues of the drawings were also published to mark the exhibitions at the Centre Georges Pompidou, Paris, in 1987, at the Musée Cantini, Marseilles, in 1995, and at the Museum of Modern Art, New York, in 1996.

(1) Interview with Paule Thévenin, Paris, July 1987.

(2) Interview with Gaston Ferdière, Aubervilliers, February 1987. Even in the last years of his life, in the late 1980s, Ferdière was still working as a psychiatrist, at the Polyclinique d'Aubervilliers, a public hospital for poor people in the northern suburbs of Paris, where I visited him on a number of occasions; he specialized there in treating children with "nervous disorders". The asylum of Rodez was closed down in 1948 – the year of Artaud's death – and the site was used for the construction of a high school, but a square in the town – the "Place Antonin Artaud" – commemorates its unwilling inhabitant. On the closure of Rodez, Ferdière opened a private clinic in south-western France, but moved back to Paris in 1961. He spent his final years writing pornography and died aged eighty-three in Hérisy, a village south of Paris, in December 1990.

(3) Max Fink, *Convulsive Therapy: Theory And Practice*, Raven Press, New York, 1979, page 159.

(4) Interview with Gaston Ferdière, Paris, March 1987.

(5) Antonin Artaud, interviewed by Jean Desternes (28 February 1948), *Le Figaro Littéraire*, Paris, 13 March 1948, page 2.

(6) Isidore Isou and Maurice Lemaître, *Antonin Artaud Torturé Par Les Psychiatres*, Éditions du Lettrisme, Paris, 1970, pages 141 and 144.

(7) Interview with Leo Navratil, Vienna, September 1986, and interview with Johann Feilacher, Klosterneuberg, February 1992; interview with Gaston Ferdière, Paris, March 1987. Navratil set up the "House of Artists" within the grounds of an Austrian asylum, the Niederrösterreichen

Krankenhaus in Klosterneuberg, near Vienna, in 1981; he retired in 1986 and his successor, Johann Feilacher, ran the "House of Artists", until 1998, when he was "re-deployed" by the asylum authorities. The "House of Artists" is open to the public.

(8) Interview with Gaston Ferdière, Aubervilliers, March 1987. The sale of the drawings was motivated, according to Ferdière, by his poverty at the time, following the closure of Rodez and his only partly successful attempts to establish a private practice.

(9) Colette Thomas (under the pseudonym "René"), *Le Testament De La Fille Morte*, Éditions Gallimard, Paris, 1954, page 151.

(10) Ferdière himself noted this dual resemblance. He also remembered that Artaud was intent on incessantly reworking the drawing until he would have obliterated the image of the face (and would then have thrown the drawing away, according to Ferdière); he asked Artaud to give him the drawing as a present (which he later sold), and credited himself with having thereby saved it. Interview with Gaston Ferdière, Manchester, May 1990.

(11) Jean Dequeker, *Naissance De L'Image* (1950), collected in *Artaud Vivant*, ed. O. Virmaux, Oswald Éditeur, Paris, 1980, pages 155–156.

(12) Interview with Paule Thévenin, Paris, July 1987.

(13) Jacques Prevel, *En Compagnie D'Antonin Artaud*, Flammarion, Paris, 1994, page 171. The young poet Jacques Prevel kept a journal of all of his many meetings with Artaud in Paris; it was made into a film, starring Sami Frey as Artaud, in 1993. The British-born Jany de Ruy was Prevel's girlfriend.

(14) Antonin Artaud, letter to André Breton, first draft, 28 February 1947, *L'Ephémère*, Paris, issue 8, winter 1968, page 5.

(15) Antonin Artaud, *Le Théâtre De La Cruauté* (November 1947), in *Oeuvres Complètes*, Volume XIII, Éditions Gallimard, 1974, page 118.

(16) Antonin Artaud, commentary (April 1946) on the drawing *La Mort Et L'Homme*, in *Oeuvres Complètes*, Volume XXI, 1985, page 233.

(17) Antonin Artaud, commentary (February 1946) on the drawing *La Maladresse Sexuelle De Dieu*, in *Oeuvres Complètes*, Volume XX, 1984, page 173.

(18) Antonin Artaud, commentary (September 1945) on the drawing *Couti L'Anatomie*, in *Oeuvres Complètes*, Volume XVIII, 1983, page 73.

(19) Antonin Artaud, *Dix Ans Que Le Langage Est Parti* (April 1947), in *Antonin Artaud, Dessins*, Éditions du Centre Georges Pompidou, Paris, 1987, page 22.

(20) ibid, page 22.

(21) The organization of the Galerie Pierre event, as well as the poor quality of the unillustrated exhibition catalogue, give the distinct impression that Artaud was treated insensitively by Pierre Loeb. Their arrangement was that Artaud had to forfeit a number of his drawings to the gallery in return for being given the exhibition, which took place during the summer holiday season. The framing, hanging and removal of the drawings appears to have been done with little care, and a number of drawings – including a portrait of Paule Thévenin – were stolen from the gallery during the hanging, never to reappear.

(22) Antonin Artaud, *Le Visage Humain* (June 1947), in *Antonin Artaud, Dessins*, page 48.

(23) ibid, page 50.

(24) Antonin Artaud, *L'Arve Et L'Aume Suivi De 24 Lettres À Marc Barbezat* (letter of 21 August 1947), L'Arbalète Éditeur, Décines, 1989, page 82.

(25) Balthus speaking in the film **Balthus The Painter**, directed by Mark Kidel and transmitted on BBC2's "Omnibus" programme, 1997.

(26) Antonin Artaud, *Exposition Balthus À La Galerie Pierre* (1934), in *Oeuvres Complètes*, Volume II, 1973, page 287.

(27) Antonin Artaud, *Balthus* (February 1947), in the catalogue *Balthus*, Éditions du Centre Georges Pompidou, Paris, 1983, page 47.

(28) Antonin Artaud, *Van Gogh Le Suicidé De La Société* (January–March 1947), Éditions Gallimard, 1990 (illustrated edition), page 81. In his essay, Artaud derides and insults a sexually obsessed psychiatrist, designated as "docteur L.", whom he had encountered during his incarceration. The doctor who had helped Ferdière to administer Artaud's electroshock treatments at Rodez, Jacques Latrémolière, claimed in the early 1960s that he was the target of Artaud's anger here, but Paule Thévenin comments in her notes to this edition of the essay that Artaud told her that the target of his wrath was actually the infamous psychoanalyst Jacques Lacan.

(29) ibid, page 110.

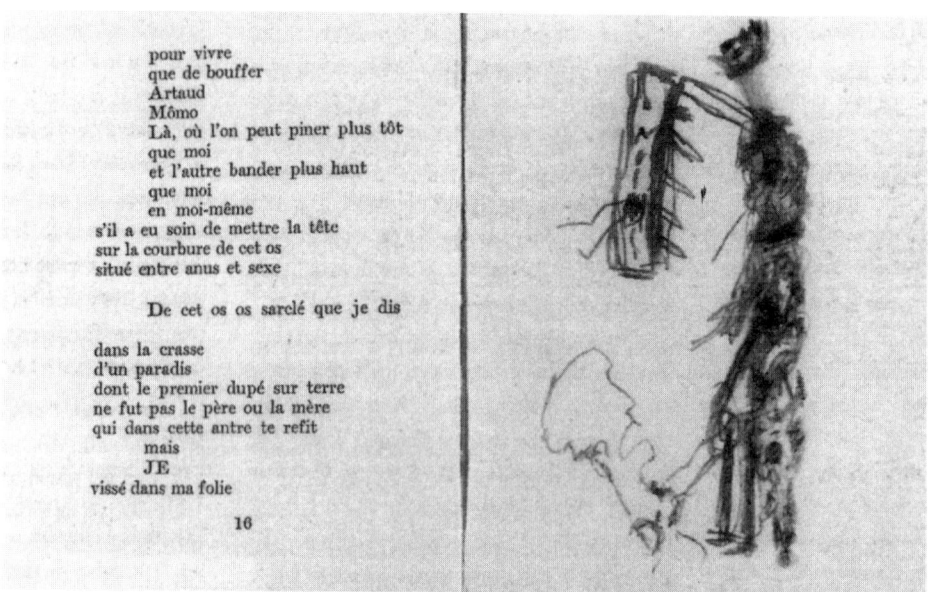

Pages from *Artaud Le Mômo*

(30) Antonin Artaud, *50 Dessins Pour Assassiner La Magie* (January 1948), in the catalogue *Antonin Artaud: Oeuvres Sur Papier,* Musée Cantini, Marseilles, 1995, page 63.

(31) Artaud did succeed in including eight pages of images and texts from his notebooks as a plate section within his book of poems, *Artaud Le Mômo*, which was published in 1947 as a small, luxuriously printed edition by Bordas Éditeur in Paris. Artaud had initially attempted to persuade Pablo Picasso to illustrate his poems, but finally decided that he would use his own notebook pages, since, as he wrote in an unpublished letter to the publisher Pierre Bordas on 6 February 1947: "Picasso would never be able to understand me as I understand myself." In the same letter, he describes the content of his notebook pages as "totems... mysterious operating machines". (The manuscript letters of Artaud's correspondence with Bordas are stored in the "Grande Réserve" section of the National Library in Paris.)

Three

The Screaming Body: Artaud's Sound Recordings 1946–48

Artaud's work in recordings – created over two short spans of time at the beginning and end of his final period of freedom in Paris – is an intense visualization of the human body. At this extreme point in Artaud's work, the body is compelled to become visual material: its appearance is the result of a disciplined but ferocious invocation. The last of Artaud's recordings – *To Have Done With The Judgement Of God* – forms a vast project for physical transformation: a project that uneasily inhabited the medium of the radio broadcast, which Artaud adopted as the sole means that would enable him to transmit his work to a mass audience. In sound alone, the visual body is integrally absent, and Artaud's screaming body is an intricate amalgam of linguistic and physical elements that counter that absence of the body, while enforcing its materialization explicitly for a large audience. Where Artaud's drawings were seen publicly by only a small number of friends and exhibition-goers during the weeks in which they were installed at the Galerie Pierre, his recorded work was intended to be experienced by an audience of millions.

Radio played a powerful and dominant role in the lives of virtually all of the citizens of Paris (and throughout France and Europe) in the years after the Second World War. An evening programme on the national radio station – which, while nominally independent, was under the indirect control of the French government – would invariably have a huge and indiscriminate audience. In addition to news bulletins and reports, the content of a night's broadcasting would typically range from crass entertainment quiz programmes, to medical and psychological advice programmes, to programmes of work by poets, writers and musicians, including those associated with the Parisian avant-garde movements (even under the German Occupation, experiments in radio as an innovative art form had continued to flourish). As a medium for the dissemination of information, entertainment and culture to a mass audience within the home, radio was pre-eminent. In this sense, Artaud's recordings – conceived within the context of the late 1940s French radio system – are popular culture of an utterly shattering and unique kind.

In the case of the last of his recordings, Artaud's work was suppressed in its entirety (by the radio station which had commissioned it, rather than by a governmental body, although the border between the two institutions was blurred). That final recording is Artaud's most advanced and furious work on the human body. It is also the work in which he most strategically and actively aimed to elude the process of representation: a process that he had railed against in his film writings, and combatted with fury in his drawings. For Artaud, it is representation alone which makes the body absent. Into the process of representation are subsumed the forces of society, religion, psychiatry and medicine in general, and also the work of censorship which summarily prevented the broadcasting of Artaud's work – a broadcast which he perceived literally to be a physical transmission. On a further level, the recording is a highly sociological denunciation – accentuated by an element of hallucination – of the consumer culture of post-war France and, especially, of the United States' use of Cold War hysteria to assimilate Europe to its political, military and cultural influences. This was the era of the Marshall Plan and its economic subjugation of parts of Europe, including France, to the domination (simultaneously both financial and cultural) of the United States. And Artaud's last work, finally, is theology of a virulent and pure kind – an anti-religious language of the scream made new, vivid flesh.

On his return to Paris in May 1946, Artaud had no plans for recordings. His projects for gaining a mass audience for his work were focused on his desire to publish it in mass-circulation newspapers such as *Combat*. But although several short extracts from his work in progress would indeed appear in that newspaper, which was under the direction of Albert Camus and Pascal Pia during Artaud's final period in Paris, he came to perceive it as an inadequate site for his work. In the format of the newspaper, Artaud's preoccupations were swamped; and the intrinsically temporal and fixed nature of a newspaper clashed reductively with Artaud's aim for an expanding, launching space for his attacks and for the incessant transmutations of his work. His adoption of the radio recording as an alternative space for this work occurred through an outside intervention. He made the first of his recordings for radio in the month following his return to Paris, at the moment when he was still about to resume his drawing work, with the first sequence of facial portraits that were begun in that summer. The producer of a programme devoted to innovations in radio form, "New Experiments Club", had sent Paule Thévenin to Artaud's pavilion in Ivry-sur-Seine to request a contribution from him (this was Thévenin's first meeting with Artaud). He was initially reluctant, his prescient suspicion being that the medium of radio was not one which would give him the freedom to express exactly what he wanted to. But, since he immediately liked and trusted Paule Thévenin, he agreed to her request. On 8 June, Artaud recorded a text he had written especially for the occasion, entitled *The Patients And The Doctors*; it was transmitted on the following day.

The text denounces his treatment in the asylums of France, and offers a radical reworking of definitions of health and sickness. The text polemically demands a reversal of the positions of the doctor and the patient. For Artaud, the person who is ill has experienced the hideous beauty of life. This experience gives the patient the absolute right of access to drugs such as heroin and cocaine. In the aural space of the recording, Artaud's voice grates and grinds over his words and glossolaliac exclamations, which are hammered and whistled out of his body and mouth. But, on listening back to the recording, Artaud was unhappy with what he saw as its ponderous speed and heaviness. He decided to record another text, and the radio programme agreed to transmit it. This second recording, *Madness And Black Magic*, recorded on 16 July and transmitted on the following day, dealt with the tortuous absence of identity experienced by the awakening electroshock patient. This recording accuses the French psychiatric hospitals of magical

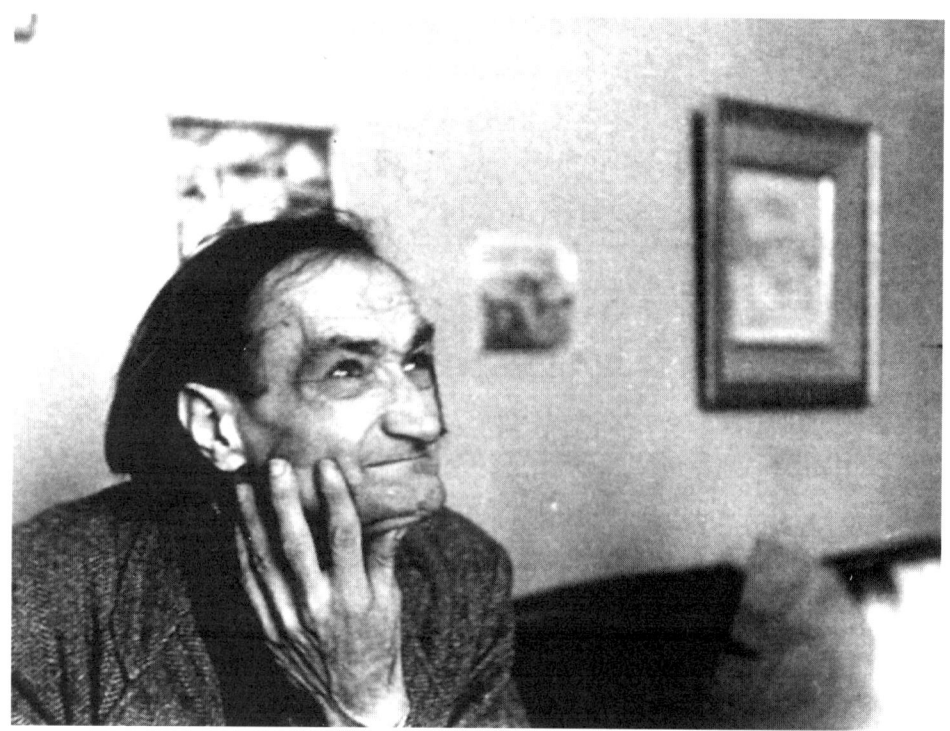

Artaud at Ivry, 1947

practices that involve the sexual butchery and robbery of patients' bodies while they are held vulnerable and defenceless through such treatments as insulin shock comas and electroshock comas. Skinned naked in a bath of electricity, each electroshock patient is exposed to an artificially-created death – and at this stage in Artaud's work, all manifestations of death are states of black magic that have to be overturned. Again, Artaud was unhappy with his work as it appeared within the medium of radio, and abandoned the form for the next sixteen months.

At the beginning of November 1947, Artaud received an invitation from the radio programme "The Voice Of The Poets" to prepare a broadcast on whatever subject he wanted. His broadcast was intended to form the first of a new series of works which the programme's editor, Fernand Pouey, had instigated. Most of the textual material for *To Have Done With The Judgement Of God*, as Artaud entitled his project, was written urgently, within the space of two weeks, since the main part of the recording sessions had been scheduled for the end of the same month. Artaud chose three collaborators to work with him on the project: Roger Blin, Maria Casarès and Paule Thévenin.[1] Casarès had replaced Artaud's original choice, the actress Colette Thomas, who found the project too exhausting and suddenly withdrew from participating in it. Artaud prepared his collaborators intensively but very briefly: the texts to be performed had only one rehearsal, on 22 November. All of the material was performed and recorded on 29 November in the salubrious studios of the French national radio station, in a highly tense atmosphere which Paule Thévenin remembered as one of "violence".[2] Both she and Casarès were deeply disturbed by the demands of their contributions to the recording; only the more ironical and detached Roger Blin was able to take the session more in his stride. What Artaud called the *bruitages* or "noise effects" of the recording – screams, cries, dialogues in invented language, percussion and bangs – were then recorded by Artaud, together with Blin, on 16 January 1948, and edited into the pre-existent material. The date of the recording's transmission (which was to be only in the Parisian region, not throughout France) was set for 2 February.

Artaud's final recording is a polyphony of screams and language, of assonant and obtuse rhythms, of insurgent elements of chance, and of outbursts of a black, apocalyptic laughter which mocks religion. In its projection of imageries of the human body with sound alone, the work recalls Artaud's declarations about the presence of sound at his Studio 28 lecture on the nature of cinema, almost twenty years earlier. As Artaud had emphasized then, in 1929, sound underlines its real inhabitation and fracturing of space as it engulfs the room in which it is heard, creating its own visual emanation; in Artaud's recording from 1947–48, sound is the real mark of the body. During the final stage of his involvement with cinema, with his film project *The Butcher's Revolt*, Artaud had explored the potential for an arrhythmic collision of sound elements against the film image and its space, resulting in a hostile and compulsive impact on the spectator. In *To Have Done With The Judgement Of God*, sound works as both aural and visual assault, with the virulence and precision of Artaud's vivid language acting as the propellant for the visual component. The recording constitutes Artaud's

POUR EN FINIR avec le jugement DE DIEU
par Antonin Artaud.

ultimate struggle with language – the interrogation, the fragmentation and the concentration of language to discover a way of viscerally conveying the body through language.

Although Artaud wanted to shorten the completed recording on listening back to it, the work otherwise met with his complete approval. He asserted that it accomplished his aim of meshing the body with language, and he believed that the resulting work would be experienced by the spectator's entire nervous system. The recording's "noise effects" are interspersed throughout its five textual elements. The long first section of the recording is performed by Artaud himself, and denounces American capitalism and imperialism: it deals with an imagined American government practice of stockpiling sperm from schoolboys, to be used to generate soldiers in the future – for the financially-motivated Cold War, a mutually beneficial confrontation between Stalinist Russia and the United States. It is to be a conflict of simulation, bluffs and artifice. Artaud's voice tears at his words, hysterically and coldly humorous. The second text, *Tutuguri, The Ritual Of The Black Sun*, performed by Maria Casarès, details the dance of the Tarahumara Indians which Artaud had watched in the isolated northern mountains of Mexico in 1936; in Artaud's interpretation of the dance within the preoccupations of his recording, it serves to exact the abolition of the Christian cross and the institution of a new, physical sign which negates religion and is uniquely forged from bleeding flesh, cries and violence. The third text, *The Search For Fecality*, performed by Roger Blin, projects an imagery of excrement posed against bone; the text taunts human beings for having cowardly bodies of soft, pliable meat when "to live,/you have to be somebody,/to be somebody,/you have to have a BONE,/and not be afraid of showing the bone,/and losing the meat in the process."[3] Excrement and "god", together with all thoughts and ideas which enter or leave the body, are excess organs for Artaud. He denounces all languages and signs which betray and lose themselves within the pull of time and in the repetitious process of representation – in his notes written during his preparations for the recording, Artaud had noted: "I abject all signs. I create only machines of instant utility."[4] His text affirms that an army has now revolted to end the judgement of "god" by creating a body totally without organs: a tree of walking will. The fourth part of the recording is performed by Paule Thévenin. This text, *The Urgent Question...*, attacks the status and prestige accorded to ideas (elsewhere, Artaud wrote that ideas are only the voids of the body), and examines the concept of "the infinite" as a liberatory gesture, rather than as an idea: "the infinite", for Artaud, is "the *opening*/of our consciousness/towards possibility/beyond measure."[5] Artaud performed the recording's closing text. He cuts across his own voice, assuming the interrupting voice of his spectators as they yell for him to be placed back in a strait-jacket. Artaud's own voice obstinately breaks through, with a final imagery of the reconstruction of the human body on an autopsy table: Artaud's act of radical anatomy will excise "god" and the body's organs, ultimately instigating a delirious, wrong-way-round dance of disciplined will to be undertaken by that human body.

In the days before the anticipated transmission of his recording on 2 February 1948, Artaud asserted that it would work to attack and jolt the people of Paris, but would also bring to them deliverance and "corporeal glory"[6]. He especially wanted the recording to impact upon and provoke those engaged in hard, poorly-salaried manual work, such as metalworkers and road-menders. But then, the day before its expected transmission, the recording was banned as inflammatory and obscene by the head of the radio station. "It was banned just as though it were a porno movie," as Paule Thévenin said.[7] On the evening of 2 February, with supreme irony, Parisian listeners to the radio heard a broadcast about how the city's inhabitants needed, in the era of the Marshall Plan, to be aware of American popular culture and to adapt their lives to it. Despite newspaper scandals and private auditions of Artaud's recording – at which writers such as Jean Cocteau and Paul Éluard declared that it should be transmitted – the ban stayed in place. With the exception of a handful of clandestine copies, such as those belonging to Paule Thévenin (who retained a copy of the unedited material) and Roger Blin, the recording disappeared for forty years. Artaud was enraged at the censorship, which he perceived as being essentially linked to representation itself as allied processes of social sabotage, and wrote that "wherever the *machine* is/there is always the abyss, nothingness."[8] Now, after this last disaster, he declared that he would create what he called "a theatre of blood"[9] with terminal violence. Just over one month after the ban on his work, and ill with intestinal cancer, he died on 4 March in his pavilion at Ivry-sur-Seine, having taken an overdose of chloral hydrate.

The scream is the core of Artaud's recording: it emerges from, projects, and visualizes the body. In the space of the recording, the interaction between Artaud's scream and the silences which surround it work to generate a volatile and tactile material of sound, image and absence. Artaud placed and juxtaposed the elements of the work with extreme attention – everything, he wrote, was arranged "at a hairsbreadth/in a fulminating order".[10] The multiple eruptions and intersections at work in Artaud's language tear apart all residues of narrative and temporal flow, constructing a framework for the body which exists on multiple spatial levels. Voices emerge from behind voices in dense trajectories of sound which move and act in an infinite number of directions. It is within this projection of a language executed in a swarm of screams, words and chance elements – in an overwhelming rush and beating of sound – that Artaud creates an explicit awareness of his own *return* from the silence and physical incapacitation of his incarceration of nine years in the asylums of France. The intention of that return of Artaud's language with the body is to collide sensationally with the structures of the French language – and with the nature of language itself – so irreparably fracturing and forcibly reinventing them.

The power of laughter to negate and refuse is deeply involved in Artaud's language. Laughter works as both an explosive attack and as a corrosive taunting. Artaud's outraged derision in his recording for the badly-formed and cowardly human body compounds the ridicule he aims at the ludicrous definition of irrecoverable insanity which had been imposed upon him by a succession of psychiatrists, from Jacques Lacan to Gaston Ferdière. On another level, Artaud's laughter is a violent probing of signification, exploring and digging into the repeatable, assimilable face of language, and cancelling it out. This anatomy of language reveals the disunified, multiplicitous body in language which Artaud puts in the place of what he views as the social language of representation, with its malicious urge to fix and to define. Artaud's language breaks out in irrationally pulsing movements; it transforms, contradicts and destroys whatever it encounters. But Artaud's laughter is intentional as well as wild; however convulsively out-of-control it may seem to go, it always remains absolutely at the service of Artaud's struggle for the human body. His work, he declares, "isn't the symbol of an absent void,/of an appalling incapacity for man to realize himself in life./It is the affirmation/of a terrible/and moreover inescapable necessity."[11]

The perpetual focus of that sense of necessity is the body. Artaud's work positively concerns little else. It is his obsession. The aim of his recording is to erase all of its own temporal gaps and voids, in order for the body it evokes to be transmitted immediately and physically. Alongside Artaud's screams and his dense, controlled words, only silences can survive in this language, so that the body can breathe them. Language starts with the body and hits back against the body; in order for it to become infinite, the body's action must bypass the mental processes which Artaud despises. He writes: "The act I'm talking about aims for the true organic and physical transformation of the human body."[12] In order to validate an existence for the body, Artaud must reduce language and reduce corporeal matter to an extreme essence. Everything extraneous to the body is refused – all nature and all culture – so that the body is by itself, sharpened, bone and nerve, without family, "god" or internal organs. It can also move before itself in space, in order to create and generate itself. It is unprecedented and has no progenitor. Artaud's language in *To Have Done With The Judgement Of God* is reduced and pared: it is burnt into the body, to express this need for physical self-responsibility. Everything in the recording must emerge into auditory space at once, and this entails an intense and aggressive process of reduction which strongly recalls the demands of Artaud's film writings for an absolute density in the image. And as with his polemics for a new kind of cinema, Artaud's recorded work exacts a magnetic, inescapable welding of itself with its spectator. In his recording, Artaud sets out a physical act for his spectators which will radically transform the human body (and, by implication, the spectators' own bodies); but, through its participation in this upheaval, the body will have created for itself a unique will. Similarly, Artaud's language itself is fragmented, but its screaming desire for physical transmission sutures the pieces back together again in the spectators' bodies, where they can transform themselves.

In his pavilion at Ivry-sur-Seine, Artaud worked to generate an open-ended, violent language which involved the production of dancing, fighting, incanting, hacking with a hammer at a huge block of wood, writing, drawing: all of these connecting elements being conducted and explored to the point of exhaustion. The scream is what is forced out of all of these elements together, at once; it is simultaneously soldered out of diverse materials and made to burst out into the atmosphere. Its components collapse together to propel it. The infinity of the body is in the voice. All of the areas of the body used in Artaud's work – especially the hand and the vocal tract – are concentrated and splintered up into the scream. Then the voice attacks, acts back on what Artaud sees as the betraying organs of the body. The scream is a very dark area, far away from normal or everyday language, but as Artaud emphasized in 1947: "All true language is incomprehensible."[13]

The dancing body was always a strong image for Artaud in his work. The last words of his recording evoke the dancing bodies of young Parisians engaged in an erotic frenzy in the popular dance-halls of the time. His own scream is itself an exploratory dancing of the extremities of the body. Artaud wrote extensively about dance in his final months, emphasizing a dance of furious revolt which could be brought into existence in order to detonate "the misery of the human body".[14] Dance, for Artaud, can negate "god". And dance is also the point of origin for a transformation of the human body, through a violent but self-controlled exploration of itself and its potential exposure to elements of chance and external attack. Dance is how the body patrols, tests and defends itself from obliteration: so, the body engaged in this act must by essence be distorted, painful and alert – as well as in ecstasy at its own movements and gestures. As Tatsumi Hijikata – the Japanese inventor of the seminal "Butoh" dance performance art of the 1960s, and the only artist ever to have advanced Artaud's work – understood, the scream is the end point of dance; the scream exerts an exactly choreographed image of the body with all its extremes of sensation.[15]

The scream is a compulsive act of falling, inducing a moment at which the awareness of the body's necessity is made to develop. As far back as the mid-1930s, Artaud had written: "I fall./I fall but I am not afraid./I bring up my fear in the noise of rage.../to scream I must fall./I fall into an underworld and I cannot get out, I can never get out.../This scream I've thrown out is a dream./But a dream which eats the dream."[16] The scream spills out over whatever defines it, to become dangerous. And finally, the scream is Artaud's dense language – the tearing apart of meaning and representation, and the only way to project his authentic body.

In Artaud's work, the scream is made a visual, physical substance in space. The human fascination with visualizing and materializing the scream – as both a primary obsession and an artistic preoccupation – is so compelling as to be without an origin, unless the very process of making images of the human body can be assigned an origin. In the first known cave paintings of the human figure, the face cries in triumph or pain; in the first icons of the figure of Christ being crucified, the mouth opens in torment or ecstasy. The pre-eminent images of the scream, for contemporary art, are those painted by Edvard Munch between 1893 and 1895, and by Francis Bacon in the late 1940s. For Munch, in *The Scream*, the scream was an image that encompassed the essential substance of human experience, in its reaction to a natural world whose spectacular transformation from sky into blood, over the city of Oslo at sunset, transmits hostility and the imminence of death to its horrified witness. Munch's image of the scream is the border, to be approached with trepidation, between malevolent nature and human madness, anguish and death. Notably, Munch was intensely preoccupied with juxtaposing his image of the scream with language, in the form of a fragmentary text that caught and allied itself to the same experience; over many years, he produced numerous versions of this text, one variant of which reads: "I walked along the road with two friends – /and the sun went down/The sky suddenly became blood – and I felt/as if a breath of sadness/I stopped – leaned against the railing/tired to death/Over the blue-black fjord and city lay clouds of dripping/steaming blood/My friends walked on and I was left in/fear with an open wound in my breast./a great scream went through nature".[17]

Francis Bacon painted the human scream in around the same years that Artaud was executing his own scream, in particular with his *Figure Study II* of 1945–1946 and his sequence of screaming figures from the late 1940s inspired by Velazquez's portrait of Pope Innocent X. At that time, Bacon's imageries of the human scream were thought of as responses – involuntary or intentional – to the warfare of the preceding years and its concentration camps, mass exterminations and revelation of potential nuclear annihilation. But Bacon's avowed intention, made clear in his interviews with David Sylvester, was to create the most beautiful image of the scream, with glorious

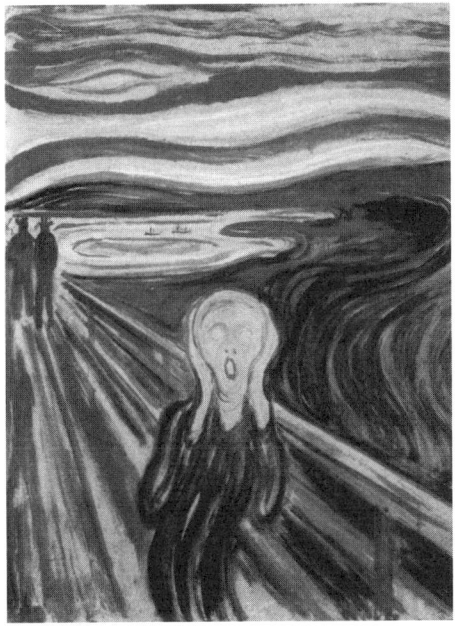

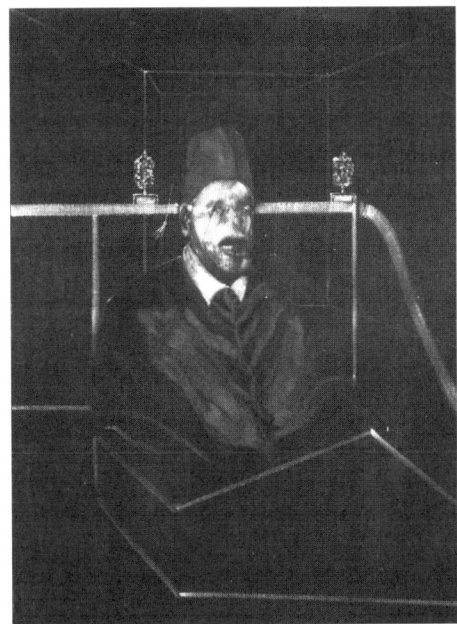

Edvard Munch, *The Scream*, 1893   Francis Bacon, *Study Number Six After*

bursts of colour to catch the living flesh and the movement of the mouth. In this aim, he explicitly distanced himself from Munch's exploration of human experience. Bacon said: "You could say that the scream is a horrific image; in fact, I wanted to paint the scream more than the horror. I think, if I had really thought about what causes somebody to scream, it would have made the scream that I tried to paint more successful. Because I should in a sense have been more conscious of the horror that produced the scream."[18] Bacon considered that he had failed in his work on the scream; significantly, he believed that it was a black-and-white image from a film, rather than a painting or drawing, that visually conveyed the scream with the sensorial exactitude and splendour that he desired. This was a still from the Odessa steps sequence of Sergei Eisenstein's 1925 film **The Battleship Potemkin,** in which a woman's face is seen full-on, the eyes staring (one of them penetrated by a bullet which has sent her spectacles awry and shattered one lens), the mouth strained at its extreme limits, a gestural streak of blood traversing the face vertically. In John Maybury's 1998 film about the obsessions of Francis

Bacon, **Love Is The Devil**, an ejaculatory stream of vivid scarlet blood propelled from a boxing-match punch spatters across the ecstatic face of the watching Francis Bacon in an exact visual counterpart to Eisenstein's image of the Odessa woman. For Bacon, it was film – or the condensation of all film imageries into one unique still image – that visually seized the scream. He commented: "I did hope one day to make the best painting of the human cry. I was not able to do it and it's much better in the Eisenstein and there it is."[19] Where Munch and Bacon painted the scream, and Eisenstein filmed it, Artaud's work is uniquely the scream itself: the visceral and visual transmission of the body: breath, blood, saliva, sperm, bone.

All of Artaud's visual work is a wild but disciplined concoction of images, languages and screams. At a late stage in this work, Artaud had given emphasis to the invented language of his glossolalia as embodying the point of intersection between these three elements. The glossolalia, as an incantation of invented words and sounds, were developed sonically, as a testing of the body's capacities, and were then transferred to the surface of the page or drawing, poised between a textual language and a visual arrangement. Artaud placed the dense lines of his glossolalia figuratively in the centre of the page's surface (insisting that, in their printed form, they should be further emphasized visually through being printed in bold characters), or else at a highlighted point of his drawing's surface space.

To the end of his work, Artaud was preoccupied with creating a visual language which, at their diverse stages, his film projects and his drawings embody. Artaud's drawings, especially, are an interrogation of the surface – the paper which he assaulted, sliced and burned – and its potential to hold and show the gestures and existence of the body. But, at the extreme point of his work, the use of a surface is abandoned, and his visual work – the scream, that, for Artaud, carries the body and negates its representation – is projected directly onto and into space, endlessly.

Artaud's screaming body is the violent revelation of all the raw extremities of existence.

NOTES

All of Artaud's recorded work – with the exception of a small number of "out-takes" from *To Have Done With The Judgement Of God* – is available in the form of a boxed set of compact discs issued by André Dimanche Éditeur, Marseilles, in 1995. A single compact disc of *To Have Done With The Judgement Of God* was also issued in 1995 by Sub Rosa Aural Documents, Brussels. The whole of the text of *To Have Done With The Judgement Of God*, together with Artaud's working notes and letters about the recording, appears in French (as *Pour En Finir Avec Le Jugement De Dieu*) in the Gallimard edition of the *Oeuvres Complètes*, Volume XIII (Paris, 1974). An excellent translation by Clayton Eshleman of all of the text of *To Have Done With The Judgement Of God* appears in his collection of Artaud translations entitled *Watchfiends And Rack Screams: Works From The Final Period* (published by Exact Change Press, Boston USA, 1995). Eshleman, who devoted many years to his translations, is the only translator to have created an accurate English-language counterpart for Artaud's language; virtually all other volumes of translations of Artaud's work are erroneous and should be avoided like the plague.

(1) Roger Blin (1907–1984) was, at the time, a film and theatre actor (and former left-wing political activist) who was in the process of making the transition to becoming a prominent theatre director; a close friend of Artaud's since the late 1920s, he would go on to direct vastly influential first productions of works by Samuel Beckett and Jean Genet. Maria Casarès (1922–1996) was, by this time, already renowned as one of the outstanding actresses of her generation, having worked with film directors such as Robert Bresson and Marcel Carné, as well as in the theatre; she would appear, two years later, as the "Princess of Death" in Jean Cocteau's film **Orphée**. Paule Thévenin (1922–1993) was a former medical student who was then working, unpaid, as Artaud's assistant.

(2) Interview with Paule Thévenin, Paris, September 1988.

(3) Antonin Artaud, *Pour En Finir Avec Le Jugement De Dieu*, in *Oeuvres Complètes*, Volume XIII, Éditions Gallimard, Paris, 1974, page 84.

(4) Working notes (November 1947) towards *Pour En Finir Avec Le Jugement*

De Dieu, page 273.

(5) *Pour En Finir Avec Le Jugement De Dieu*, pages 91–92.

(6) Antonin Artaud, letter to Wladimir Porché, 2 February 1948, *Oeuvres Complètes*, Volume XIII, page 131.

(7) Interview with Paule Thévenin, Paris, March 1987.

(8) Antonin Artaud, letter to Paule Thévenin, 24 February 1948, *Oeuvres Complètes*, Volume XIII, page 146.

(9) ibid, page 146.

(10) Introductory note (November 1947) to *Pour En Finir Avec Le Jugement De Dieu*, page 69.

(11) Antonin Artaud, *Le Théâtre De La Cruauté* (a text from November 1947, intended to be recorded as part of *Pour En Finir Avec Le Jugement De Dieu*, but excluded due to time constraints), *Oeuvres Complètes*, Volume XIII, page 110.

(12) Antonin Artaud, *Le Théâtre Et La Science* (July 1947), *L'Arbalète*, Décines, issue 13, summer 1948, page 15.

(13) Antonin Artaud, *Ci-Gît* (November 1946), *Oeuvres Complètes*, Volume XII, 1974, page 95.

(14) *Le Théâtre De La Cruauté*, page 116.

(15) At least in its original form of the 1960s, Tatsumi Hijikata's "Ankoku Butoh" ("Dance Of Utter Darkness"), accords exactly with Artaud's ultimate conception of the dancing human body in a state of violent self-interrogation, traversed simultaneously by sensations of ecstasy and annihilation. Much of the initial imagery of Butoh emerged from the devastated Tokyo of the end of the Second World War, during which tens of thousands of the city's inhabitants had been reduced to ashes by American and British firebombing, leaving only a few fragments of surviving buildings – such a complete return to zero necessarily resulted in a crucial sensation of liberation and sexual experimentation, manifested in Tokyo's extreme forms of art, film and sex of the ensuing riotous decades. Hijikata (1928–1986), a close collaborator of other Japanese 1960s avant-garde legends such as Shuji Terayama, Eikoh Hosoe, Kazuo Ohno and Tadanori Yokoo, read Artaud's work assiduously as soon as it appeared in Japanese translation; another of his vital preoccupations was with the dolls created by Hans Bellmer. In 1971, he wrote an essay on Artaud entitled *Artaud's Slipper*, but this intense

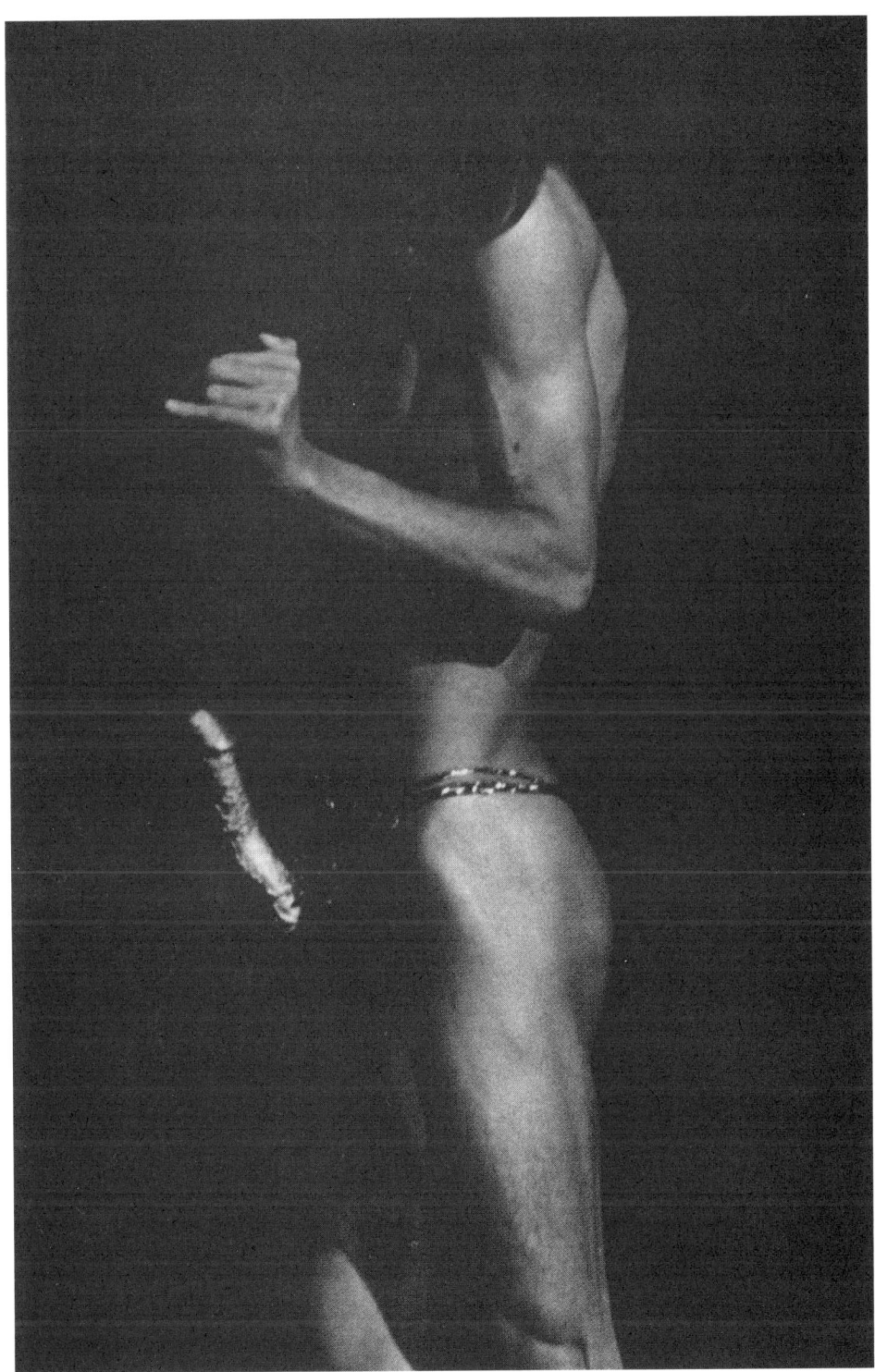

Tatsumi Hijikata, *Revolt Of The Flesh*

engagement with Artaud's work primarily manifested itself in his dance performances such as *Revolt Of The Flesh* (1968) and *Story Of Smallpox* (1972), and in his filmic and photographic collaborations with Eikoh Hosoe, who was also responsible for the infamous book of photographs of Yukio Mishima, *Killed By Roses*, from 1963, in which Mishima's body is depicted in erotic contortions of bondage and torture. In 1984, Hijikata heard Artaud's recording *To Have Done With The Judgement Of God*, which the writer Kuniichi Uno had brought back from Paris, where he had been collaborating with Gilles Deleuze. As a result, Hijikata worked on a performance based in part on *To Have Done With The Judgement Of God* with the choreographer Min Tanaka, but both were dissatisfied with the result. Hijikata was formulating a new work based on his engagement with Artaud and his own revolutionary conception of the human body in crisis, tentatively entitled *Experiment With Artaud*, when he suddenly died of liver failure in Tokyo in January 1986 (much of his work towards the project had entailed five-day non-stop drinking bouts in the labyrinthine bar districts of Tokyo as he formulated his ideas with Uno). In February 1998, Min Tanaka undertook a series of three unique performances in Tokyo based on Artaud's scenario *The Conquest Of Mexico*, which undoubtedly marked the most astonishing choreographic experiment with Artaud's work to date. Interviews with Eikoh Hosoe, Min Tanaka, Akiko Motofuji, Kuniichi Uno, Tokyo, July 1997–July 1998.

(16) Antonin Artaud, *Le Théâtre De Séraphin* (a text about screaming from 1935, intended for inclusion in the collection of theatre essays, *Le Théâtre Et Son Double*, but eventually excluded), *Oeuvres Complètes*, Volume IV, 1978, pages 178–179.

(17) Edvard Munch, text (from around 1897–1898 or 1905) accompanying his sequence of works entitled *The Scream*, in Bente Torjusen, *Words And Images Of Edvard Munch*, Thames and Hudson, London, 1989, page 136.

(18) Francis Bacon, interview from May 1966, in David Sylvester, *The Brutality Of Fact: Interviews With Francis Bacon*, Thames and Hudson, London, 1988, page 48.

(19) ibid, page 34.

index

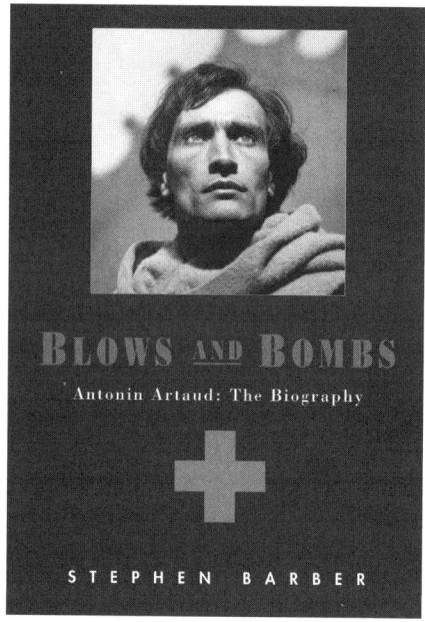